KILLER
CHEF

CHAPTER 1

IT'S A WHISPER past 10:00 p.m. in New Orleans' famous French Quarter, but it might as well be the middle of the day. The narrow streets are bustling with tipsy tourists and locals alike. Cars share their lanes with horse-drawn carriages. From every bar and club waft the sounds of clinking glasses and tinkling jazz, filling the hot night air.

A stone's throw from the banks of the Mississippi, near leafy Jackson Square, sits a food truck emblazoned with a skull and crossbones. More accurately, a *shrimp* and crossbones. Killer Chef, as it's called, is one of the most popular chuck wagons in the entire city, and for very good reason. Its po' boys are to die for.

The line for Killer Chef is always around the block, and always a good time. Jugglers and fire-breathers pace up and down, entertaining the hungry masses for tips. Passing musicians often stop and play impromptu concerts, while Gypsy psychics set up tarot card tables on the sidewalk to tell fortunes. ("I see…an incredible meal in your future.")

Tonight, the line is twice its normal length, thanks to the small army of gaffers, makeup artists, and camera operators standing in it. A film crew is in the neighborhood shooting a new romantic thriller starring one of Hollywood's biggest celebrity power couples. The crowd is desperate for a glimpse of them walking from the set to their trailer. When they smile and wave, everyone goes nuts.

Everyone, that is, except for another perfect pair: the Killer Chef co-owners, working furiously inside the truck. They stay squarely focused on their food, cranking out their legendary sandwiches with gusto.

Caleb Rooney is six two, slender and sinewy, flashing a megawatt smile. His chiseled good looks rival those of the leading man down the block. Next to him is Marlene DePietra, soft and petite, her frizzy mane of black hair held in place with a hot-pink scrunchie. Her plump cheeks are rosy, but she's not wearing a stitch of makeup. (She almost never does.) The heat inside the truck is just that intense.

"Order up!" Caleb shouts, sliding three Dark & Stormy sandwiches—a heavenly combo of garlic-ginger aioli drizzled atop Old New Orleans Rum-glazed pork belly—into a paper bag. He pauses for just a second to chomp down on a home-grown jalapeño from the bag in his pocket, then grabs two more loaves of French bread and slices them in half.

Looking over at Marlene, Caleb sees she's rummaging

of beef with Creole spices and tangy mayonnaise, when he feels a vibration in his pocket and hears Nicki Minaj's "Anaconda" blare.

He gives Marlene a sour look. "Did you seriously change my ringtone? Again? When did you get your little paws on my phone, woman?"

His partner cackles and shrugs. She's the big sister he never knew he wanted, but he adores her.

"Duck po' boy with a side of duck-fat fries," comes the order from a cocky production assistant who has just elbowed his way up to the truck. The crowd groans and boos at him for cutting the line, but they quiet down when he adds: "This one's for Angelina, so make it good."

"Caleb," Marlene sniffs, dropping some fresh fries into the sizzling fryer, "do you want to explain to this clueless young man that we make *all* of 'em good? Or should I?"

But she sees her partner isn't paying attention. His iPhone is wedged between his shoulder and his ear. He's wiping his hands on a dishrag and listening intently to the voice mail he's just received.

The grin is gone from his face.

"I know that look," says Marlene, her anger rising. "Don't you dare, Caleb. Not now. Not when half the city's standing in our line. You can't leave me alone!"

"I'm sorry, darlin'," Caleb says sheepishly, already heading for the door. "Really, really sorry. But it's bad. I gotta boogie. You know the drill."

And with that, he's gone.

"Damn it, Caleb!" Marlene shouts inside the empty truck.

She does know the drill. But that doesn't mean she likes it.

In a rage, she slams down her knife, and looks down at the unfinished beef sandwich on Caleb's board. She hurls it across the truck. It sticks momentarily to the wall with a dull squelch, then slides slowly all the way down.

Marlene takes a deep breath, forcing herself to calm down. Then she picks up a fresh roll and begins remaking the sandwich herself.

It's going to be a long night. Her partner won't be coming back anytime soon.

CHAPTER 2

CALEB HAS DASHED all the way down the hustle and bustle of Decatur Street before he realizes he's still wearing his stained apron. He rips it off and decides to take a shortcut he knows: a small path lined with street artists that runs behind the block's shops and eateries, including the famous Café Du Monde.

But as Caleb nears the pathway, he spots a roving zydeco band performing for a gaggle of beignet-lovers, clogging the pathway's entrance. *Shit.* He should've stuck to his typical route, but it's too late now.

Cursing under his breath, Caleb discreetly hurries through the band and spectators, pretending to shake a maraca to get to the other side. Once clear, his jog turns into a run.

He finally reaches a small parking lot near the French Market, races up to his sleek black Dodge Charger, and pops the trunk.

Stripping off his grimy T-shirt and jeans right there in

the open, he reaches for the garment bag inside. It contains a pair of brown slacks, a white button-down, and a dark striped tie. Caleb shimmies into the rumpled clothes, hops behind the wheel, and revs the engine.

Before pulling out, he removes a blue police beacon from the glove box and slaps it on his car's roof. He takes out a crescent-shaped gold NEW ORLEANS POLICE badge and clips it to his belt.

Caleb Rooney isn't just one of the city's top chefs. He's also one of its very best detectives.

Soon he's speeding back the way he came, along Decatur Street. Then he hooks a right and heads up St. Louis Street.

Weaving through the heavy traffic, his siren blaring, Caleb toots his horn and gives a quick wave as he passes Johnny's Po-Boy Restaurant. Johnny Jr. himself is out front smoking and returns the greeting with a knowing nod. Killer Chef has developed camaraderie with the owners of the city's sit-down po' boy places, especially once the word got out that he's a cop. Caleb used to fantasize about opening a real restaurant of his own someday, but he's gotten used to the speed and street cred that come only from running a hoppin' food truck.

Not that *keeping* it running is easy. Hell, no. Especially on such a crazy night. Starting to feel guilty about leaving Marlene on her own, Caleb asks Siri to call her cell.

"You better be calling to say you're on your way back!" Marlene yells into the phone without even saying hello. Her fury makes Caleb regret calling altogether.

"You know I would if I could," he says. "And I will. If I can."

"Yeah, yeah. Give it to me straight, doc."

Caleb hesitates. He hates to add to Marlene's stress. But he can't lie to her, either. She knows him too well for that.

"It's murder, honeypot. A double."

Marlene groans on the other end. They both know what that means. There's no way in hell he'll be back to finish the rush and help her clean up and close.

"Someone got killed in the Quarter, huh? Do we know 'em?"

Caleb doesn't respond.

"Come on. The least you can do is tell me where you're going."

Now Caleb *really* hesitates. In the background on the other end, he hears the sound of fries in duck oil sizzling and popping. "I'm on my way to Patsy's," he says.

"You gotta be kidding me!" Marlene exclaims.

"Take the fries out, Mar," Caleb says, hearing the crackling noises getting even louder. "Sounds like they're burning."

He's right. They are. Marlene angrily yanks out the fryer basket, dumps the burnt mess in the trash, and starts again. But first she steals a quick glance outside. She sees that, since her partner left, the line has grown even longer.

"Damnit, Caleb, you need to hurry up and get your big ass back here! I have things to do tonight. I have a life, too, you know."

Caleb screeches a right onto Burgundy Street, nearing his destination. Unsure how else to get Marlene off the phone, he uses one of his trademark tricks: making a whooshing static sound with his tongue. Juvenile, sure, but it gets the job done.

"Are you making the noise on me again? Caleb? You are, aren't you? Caleb?"

Caleb hangs up. Siri asks if he wants to call Marlene back. He doesn't.

Soon he arrives at Patsy's, a high-end restaurant in a beautiful historic building. Magnificent white Doric columns frame a tangerine-orange facade. With its elegant dining room and glorious kitchen, the place has been luring local and visiting celebrities for years. During any given dinner service, guests might encounter politicians, diplomats, athletes, and whichever movie stars are currently in town filming.

But tonight, this exceptional eatery is the scene of a horrific murder.

Two, to be exact.

And it's up to Detective Caleb "Killer Chef" Rooney to solve them.

A small crowd of onlookers has gathered outside. The trio of police cruisers Caleb saw earlier are parked in the street at sharp angles. He pulls up beside them, hops out of his Charger, and flashes his badge as he marches through the pack of gawkers toward the entrance.

Observing the chaos of diners and staff, he braces himself for what he's about to find inside.

CHAPTER 3

THE DOOR TO PATSY'S swings open. Caleb strides in, calm and commanding, leaving no doubt about who's now in charge of the scene.

He has eaten here plenty of times before, but he's never seen the ornate dining room so brightly lit. Or in such disarray. Cops stand at every doorway, interviewing clusters of anxious, well-dressed patrons, preventing them from leaving. On the far side of the dining room, a crime scene photographer is snapping pictures.

Caleb heads over, ignoring the eyes that follow him. He's barely gotten a few feet when he hears high heels clicking along the marble floor, heading his way, and a familiar woman's voice. "Thank God you came."

Caleb turns to see the restaurant's owner, Patsy De La Fontaine, coming toward him through the crowd. She's a pretty, sprightly redhead who wears a bit too much Elizabeth Taylor perfume, but it suits her. There's something both youthful and timeless about Patsy. Casual and elegant. And undeniably attractive.

"Detective Rooney at your service, ma'am," he says with a professional smile.

Ignoring his formality, Patsy flings her arms around Caleb's neck and melts into his muscular frame, an instinct born of their history. He returns the gesture, pulling her close in a familiar embrace.

"You got here just in time, Caleb," Patsy says, pulling away. "These clowns don't know what the hell they're doing."

"How are *you* doing?" he asks.

"Fine, I suppose. Given what's happened. I was on the other side of the dining room, saying hello to a few regulars. Then, all of a sudden, I heard screaming. Quite a commotion. I looked over and right there, at table 24…" Patsy blinks rapidly, growing emotional at the memory. "Those poor, poor people. I feel so awful for them."

Caleb has always admired Patsy's compassion in the cutthroat world of New Orleans fine dining. Most restaurateurs in her position would be furious if a double homicide had occurred in their establishment, terrified that it might shut them down for weeks, if not for good. But not Patsy—he notes that her only concern right now is for the victims.

"Don't worry," Caleb says, giving her slender shoulder a reassuring squeeze. "We'll take care of everything. Now, if you'll excuse me…"

He heads off again, navigating overturned chairs and

abandoned tables. He spots a few half-eaten sirloin steaks. Patsy's perfectly seasoned andouille sausages. Her acclaimed tapioca pudding. Breadbaskets holding untouched rolls.

Finally Caleb reaches table 24, and a chill dances up his spine.

As the police photographer deferentially steps aside, Caleb sees four legs sticking out with crooked feet, contorted at unnatural angles. A man and a woman, midforties, nicely attired, are both sprawled out on the marble floor on either side of their table. There's no blood. There are no visible wounds. No signs of struggle.

But the looks on their rigid faces are ghastly.

Whatever happened, Caleb thinks, however they died...*it was agonizing.*

He silently takes in the entire scene, scanning for anything out of the ordinary, any clues at all. The couple's partially eaten meal is still laid out in front of them: jambalaya, chargrilled oysters, a half-drained bottle of Chardonnay.

"Whatcha thinkin', Detective Rooney?" asks Officer Richard Ames, the first cop on the scene, waddling toward him. The buttons of his light-blue uniform strain against his beer belly. "None of the eyewits are giving *us* much to work with. Nobody saw nothin' suspicious. Initial search turned up no murder weapon, neither."

"That's because," Caleb says, "I think we're looking at it

right now." With nothing else to go on except the apparent suddenness of their deaths, Caleb has begun formulating a theory. Ames furrows his brow in confusion, so Caleb explains: "I believe these two were poisoned."

"Poison, huh?" Ames replies. Then he says with a smirk, "Maybe I'll take the missus *here* for our next anniversary, if you know what I mean. If this place is even still open."

Caleb scowls, but he knows Ames has a point with the tasteless joke. He wants Patsy's restaurant to stay afloat—almost as much as he wants to bring whoever murdered these two people to justice.

"How soon till the ME arrives?" he asks.

"The medical examiner's en route," Ames says. "Thirty minutes. Meantime, we're taking down all the bystanders' info. Getting statements. Might take a while."

"Tell the officers to take all the time they need. Before we cut 'em loose, I'd like to speak to as many witnesses as I can. Personally."

It's not that Caleb doesn't trust his colleagues; he just knows he has to be thorough. Given the facts, it's quite likely the killer had direct access to the victims' food. Which means it's also quite likely he or she is still on the premises.

Glancing around the dining room, Caleb notices Patsy bending down to pick up an overturned chair. He quickly moves to her and intervenes.

"I told you not to worry about that, Patz," he says, gently rubbing the space in between her shoulder blades before he catches himself. "We'll clean the whole place up real nice so you can open for lunch tomorrow. I promise."

"I appreciate that," Patsy answers. "But this is my restaurant. I really need to—"

Caleb moves his hand from her back to the chair and keeps it firmly by his side. "This *is* your restaurant. But right now, it's *my* crime scene."

Patsy looks unhappy, but then lights up with an idea.

"You boys must be starving! I was going to just close up for the night, but maybe I'll pop into the kitchen, have JD whip up a little gumbo for y'all."

"That's so kind of you," Caleb says, steering her away from the kitchen. "But I'm afraid we'll have to decline. I do want to pop into the kitchen for a minute myself, though."

Patsy takes the hint. "You've been trying to sneak a peek at some of my secret recipes for years. I guess tonight's your chance."

Caleb returns her grim smile. As a chef, he hates to treat a kitchen like a crime scene, but it might contain clues. He also needs to speak with the people who handled the couple's food.

Right now, all of them are prime suspects.

CHAPTER 4

JD McMULLAN, PATSY'S longtime executive chef, has shared enough good cigars and cheap whiskey over the years with Caleb to consider him a friend. But the moment the detective pushes through the kitchen's saloon-style doors, both men know that their past isn't worth a damn tonight. Not with two people lying dead.

"You think something in my food killed 'em?" JD exclaims. "Impossible! No way it could have come from my kitchen. I watch my staff like a hawk. Inspect every dish before it goes out."

"Any new hires lately?" Caleb asks, eyeing the dozen or so kitchen employees assembled in the corner, corralled by another cop, all staring back at him.

"None. Every one of these guys has been with me since the start. We're like family. I'd go to the mat for any of 'em." JD pauses to wipe his dripping brow. "A thing like this can ruin a business, you know. Imagine if two folks dropped dead after scarfing down one of your po' boys. My career's on the line here, man!"

Caleb tries to catch JD's eye, unsure if the burly man in stained chef's whites is about to start weeping or running. He thinks back to some of their late-night conversations, how JD spoke of his aspirations to star in his own Cajun cooking show one day. Would he really risk it all to commit murder?

Caleb speaks briefly with the rest of the kitchen staff in small groups, everyone from the sous-chefs to the line cooks to the sommelier to the dishwashers. All are cooperative. All seem just as sad and shaken and confused as JD. Calm, concerned, genuine. No telltale signs of a killer.

At least not yet.

Caleb returns to the dining room just in time to spot a pair of size 14 snakeskin boots clomping across the marble floor. They belong to Dr. Quincy Johnson, a gentle giant in his late forties with the Orleans Parish medical examiner's office. He sports an earnest smile, tiny tortoise-shell glasses, and a protruding belly full of gumbo and bathtub gin.

"Pleasure to see you, Detective," Quincy says.

The two men finish the sentence simultaneously: "…given the circumstances." It's an old routine between these old acquaintances—they've encountered each other at crime scenes across the city for nearly a decade. They shake hands cordially and approach the victims.

"Witnesses are saying the two began flailing their arms

and gasping for air at almost exactly the same time," Caleb says. "They both started to spasm, moaning in pain. Then they hit the ground."

Quincy dons a pair of latex gloves, removes his gold cuff links, rolls up his sleeves, and starts visually inspecting the bodies and surrounding area.

"Sounds like acute homicidal poisoning to me," he says, sucking at his teeth.

"You read my mind," Caleb replies. "I'll let you do your thing here. I want to try to talk to as many other patrons as I can before letting them go."

Working his way clockwise around the dining room, Caleb takes statements from a jittery mother and her sulky teenage daughter there for a birthday dinner she'll never forget. A slimy corporate lawyer who had come to Patsy's to impress a potential new client. A middle-aged gay man, owner of a local art gallery. A retired couple visiting from Boca. And the entire waitstaff, some of whom served the victims personally.

Caleb will have his team back at the station run each witness's name through the system. But the stories seem to check out, with no immediate red flags raised. Caleb prides himself on his knack for spotting bad guys after fifteen years on the force. Tonight he doesn't think he's met one.

Finishing up with the last witness, he notices Patsy sitting alone at the bar, halfway through what appears to be a tumbler of bourbon. An empty glass is already sitting in front of her. Caleb knows that feeling. He heads over and rubs her arm.

"You doing okay, Patz?"

Patsy turns to look at him, seeing Quincy and an assistant ME beginning to place the two victims into body bags. She shudders and tosses back the remainder of her liquor.

"Hell, Caleb. I don't know if I'll ever be."

CHAPTER 5

BEFORE HE CAN REPLY, Caleb spots a small alcove off the main dining room, one he's never noticed in all his times eating here. Behind the frosted-glass door are silhouettes—a group he hasn't seen yet or spoken with.

"What's in there?" he asks Patsy, who's just flagged down her bartender to pour her drink number three.

"*That* is what we call our Chef's Table," she explains. "A semiprivate dining room with its own side entrance, reserved for some of my most 'exclusive' clientele." Patsy hangs her head. "Who probably won't ever be coming back."

Leaving Patsy at the bar, Caleb opens the door to enter the little room. Inside he finds a gaggle of New Orleans minor celebrities standing around a few mahogany tables, chatting and sipping cocktails. Among them is the lead actress of a popular medical show set and shot in the city. A Pulitzer Prize–winning columnist from the *Times-Picayune*. A starting lineman for the Saints, about the size of a refrigerator, and his petite wife, who's a model.

In the corner, a clump of publicists and managers are pecking away at their smartphones, sweating like hookers in church. No doubt they're trying to figure out how to salvage the evening, which has quickly become a living nightmare for them and the VIPs they handle.

Caleb has barely stepped foot in the room when one of the handlers—a pushy, heavyset woman with spiky platinum-blond hair—marches over and accosts him.

"Finally, someone in charge!" she hisses. "Do you have any idea how long we've been kept waiting in here? A mob of paparazzi is setting up outside. If they snap even one single picture of any our clients leaving the scene of a *murder*—"

"I understand your concern, miss," Caleb says, staying cool and charming as always. He addresses the entire room: "On behalf of the New Orleans Police Department, I apologize to all of you for the inconvenience. And thank you for your cooperation. If I could just ask y'all a few questions, you can soon be on your—"

"Not a chance in hell, Rooney," says a nasal male voice.

Caleb recognizes it without turning around. It's more grating than nails on a chalkboard.

Tariq "the Tarantula" Bishar, a nebbish middle-management twerp from the mayor's office, has burst into the private dining room like he owns the place. His official title is Director of City Outreach and Cultural Development. The fancy title means he's in charge of wining and dining actors, directors, artists, musicians, athletes, models, and other "luminaries" to entice them to work, live, and play in the Crescent City—and keeping them happy once they're here. Tariq is a perpetual thorn in the NOPD's side, known to throw a wrench into any police investigation that might ruffle the feathers of the city's elite.

Tariq pushes past him and air-kisses the spiky-haired publicist with the attitude.

"By personal order of the Deputy Superintendent of the New Orleans Police Department," Tariq announces, puffing out his chest like a modern-day town crier, "all patrons of Patsy's eatery are requested to please vacate the premises as swiftly and discreetly as possible."

The crowd of celebs and their handlers murmur in relief and quickly start filing out of the private side entrance.

Caleb isn't a violent person, but his desire to wring Tariq's scrawny little neck is strong.

"Two people are in the next room *dead,* Tariq," he says, struggling to keep his cool. "But God forbid we inconvenience a couple of D-listers."

Tariq shrugs as he follows the last of the VIPs out. "Take it up with your superiors, Rooney. Not me. I'm just the messenger."

Caleb resists the impulse to strangle him—by popping

a jalapeño into his mouth and taking comfort in the tingly, familiar heat.

Realizing he's lost control of his crime scene, he heads back into the main dining room and notifies the officers that the rest of the diners can leave.

As the restaurant begins emptying out, Caleb looks back over at table 24. The two bodies have been removed. Crime scene techs are now placing the couple's likely poisoned, unfinished food and beverages into plastic containers for laboratory analysis. Even the tablecloth and cutlery are being tagged as evidence.

Caleb loosens the tie around his neck.

Now his work *really* begins.

CHAPTER 6

EMPTY RESTAURANTS HAVE a strange energy, a lingering imprint of the diners who laughed, cried, maybe even died at their tables. Tonight, Patsy's is no exception. Caleb walks slowly through the spacious rooms alone, waiting for the remaining officers to finish processing the crime scene. Not twenty minutes after the last of its shaken patrons have left, the tables abandoned mid-meal give the place a spooky air.

Caleb stops and looks closely at some black-and-white photos lining one of the rear hallways. Classy snapshots of New Orleans from almost a century ago: streetcars, flappers, jazz musicians. Images from the Pythian Temple roof garden. The old riverboat clubs. Raucous Mardi Gras celebrations of yore.

His eyes narrow in on one of his favorites, a photograph of a legendary performance by King Oliver and his Creole Jazz Band, probably taken around 1923. Caleb can practically hear their brassy, dazzling melodies just from looking at it.

"I'm gonna leave you that picture in my will," Patsy says.

She's standing at the other end of the hall. "Which means you might be getting it soon."

She starts walking toward him—*stumbling* toward him. Clearly those bracing drinks earlier have started to kick in.

"You'll get through this, Patz. Not that I couldn't stare at these photos of yours for hours."

Patsy shoots him a boozy smile and gives him an exaggerated once-over.

"I could stare at something else for hours."

Caleb stands a little straighter. His own eyes wander from Patsy's sultry lips to her luscious curves.

"I hate to ask you for anything else, but…could you give me a lift home?" she asks. "I could take the streetcar, but this whole mess tonight has thrown me into such a state. I'd probably fall asleep and wake up in a less than pleasant neighborhood."

Caleb was planning on offering one anyway.

"Of course. But you gotta do something for *me*. Don't seat table 24 for the next couple of days. It's bad luck."

"'Bad luck?' I didn't know you were superstitious."

"I'm not. I just guess you could say…kitchens, dining rooms, food trucks—those are my spiritual places. If anybody understands that, it's you."

Patsy takes his arm and slides her hand down to meet his.

Caleb wants to tell her he misses her. That he often still

thinks of her, their walks, their breakfasts in bed. Instead, he lifts her soft hand up to his lips and kisses it.

Patsy closes her eyes and moans softly. But Caleb breaks off their display of affection before it goes any further.

"C'mon," he says. "Let's get you out of here before a busboy catches us."

"There aren't any busboys at my place," Patsy whispers.

Caleb informs Officer Ames that he'll be stepping away from the crime scene for the night, then leads Patsy out of her restaurant and into his Charger—unsure whether to take her bait or let the heat between them fizzle out. There was always something about Patsy that made him keep his guard up.

They ride along together in silence for a few minutes until his cell phone rings—Nicki Minaj. Patsy giggles.

"Hi, Marlene."

"Get everything sorted out at that overrated madhouse yet?"

The volume is high and Marlene's voice carries. Patsy looks over at Caleb, offended. Caleb tries to defuse the situation by changing the subject.

"Did you make it through the dinner rush okay?"

As he'd hoped, this launches Marlene into a wild rant about how crazy the last ninety minutes have been, and all the cleaning and scrubbing she now has to do, *alone*.

"Yeah, but I knew you could handle it, see?" Caleb says,

buttering her up. "Look, I can't really talk right now, Mar, but I'll see you in the morning. Love you."

"I hate you. But I love you, too."

Caleb hangs up—and squirms, uncomfortable that Patsy overheard their conversation, especially that last part. She raises an eyebrow and asks with disdain and maybe a touch of jealousy, "You really still love your ex-wife?"

Caleb is actually proud of the fact that he and his ex aren't just cordial to each other but are quite close—close enough to run a successful business together.

He doesn't have to think twice. "I do."

Probably not the answer Patsy was hoping for, but she knows how important Marlene is to him, though they never got along. She flips the question around to herself. "Do you love me?"

Caleb finds this endearing. He considers the different ways the evening might go, depending on his answer, but decides to be honest.

"Marlene and I were married for years, so it's a different dynamic. But I care about you, Patsy. A whole lot."

Patsy seems to accept that response as Caleb pulls up in front of her apartment, the top floor of a quaint two-story town house in Faubourg Lafayette, where the two shared many pleasant days and steamy nights.

"Thanks again for driving me home, Detective," Patsy

says with more than a hint of flirtatiousness. She gently strokes his muscled forearm. "Now what?"

Caleb looks over at this beautiful woman. He thinks about all the things he wants, needs, but probably shouldn't act on. He's left Marlene in the lurch back at the truck. Not to mention he's got a fresh double homicide to investigate.

But Caleb decides all of that can wait.

He switches off the ignition and unbuckles his seat belt. "I could go for a nightcap. How about you?"

CHAPTER 7

PATSY'S NEIGHBORHOOD, THE Tenth Ward, is a patchwork of multifamily homes, colorful town houses, and funky shops and cafés. Her apartment sits directly above a small funeral parlor that's been in business since the 1940s. From the look of the faded, gold-stenciled lettering on its glass storefront and the peeling, lime-green wallpaper inside, it probably hasn't been renovated since then, either.

Caleb places a hand on Patsy's lower back as she leads them up the creaky wooden staircase to her front door.

As soon as she pushes it open, he breathes in the familiar scent of pinewood and incense he remembers so well. But plenty has changed about the apartment, too, since the last time he was inside. Some of the furniture's been rearranged. The walls have been freshly painted, a soothing beige with white trim.

"Place looks good, Patz," Caleb says as he crosses the threshold.

Patsy releases a pained exhale and slumps her shoulders,

bone-tired. It's as if all the stress and chaos of the night have finally caught up with her.

After a moment, she moves to a small credenza and pours two glasses of port.

"That's right," Caleb says, remembering. "You were in Portugal last month." He takes a glass of the maroon liquid from Patsy and gently swishes it. "How was your trip?"

"Wonderful. Truly. I brought back a few bottles of this amazing Garrafeira. Cheers." With a raise of her glass, she and Caleb clink. "I stayed at a château in the Douro Valley. It was beautiful. But my room was…a little lonely. You should have come."

Caleb takes a sip of the rich, fruity wine. Then he sets the glass down and moves to embrace her.

Patsy turns away from him and silently leads him into the bedroom, where they partially disrobe and slip under the covers.

But Caleb doesn't have any lusty expectations. He's intuitive enough to know that Patsy just wants him there, *needs* him there, for comfort and support, nothing more.

Patsy shuts off the light, then reaches for the remote and flips on the small TV mounted on the wall across from the bed. She navigates to the Cooking Channel and turns the volume low. Caleb remembers that she likes a bit of ambient noise when she sleeps. He pulls her tenderly into his arms. Patsy sighs deeply and within seconds dozes off.

Caleb listens to her soft, rhythmic breathing, and the sounds of a TV chef explaining the final-round challenge of a reality cooking show. But his thoughts begin to drift back to the two people murdered in Patsy's restaurant's dining room just hours earlier.

He tries to catch some winks himself, but instead his mind starts to race. There are so many questions he wants to ask his bedmate.

For starters: *"Who do you think did it?"*

The investigation has barely begun, but already Caleb's feeling frustrated. He envisions the grisly crime scene again in his head. He just can't help it. He mentally replays the dozens of brief interviews he conducted.

Could he have spoken to the killer tonight and not known it?

Outside, the evening wind is picking up a bit. The windows rattle, as if something from the world beyond is knocking, summoning Caleb, trying to let itself in.

CHAPTER 8

THE MORNING BIRDS are just starting to chirp when Caleb slips out from under Patsy's lavender sheets and tiptoes into the kitchen.

There he discovers, happily, that her fridge is fairly well stocked. He wants to start their day off on the right foot by whipping up a small feast.

Knowing Patsy to be an eggs Benedict aficionado, Caleb begins by preparing his famous mornay sauce, heating the milk and flour into a silky froth before removing the mixture from the heat and whisking in the cheese.

Patsy doesn't have any buttermilk for the traditional southern biscuits he'd hoped to bake, so Killer Chef does some killer improvising. Caleb chops a few jalapeños from his personal stash and tosses them into the dough along with a fistful of raisins, to give each bite of the biscuits the perfect balance of spicy and sweet.

Patsy pads into the kitchen just as Caleb is arranging some seared andouille slices atop the steaming biscuit halves. "Smells like heaven," she says.

But Caleb doesn't respond; he keeps his laserlike focus on his food. He slides a cooked egg on each biscuit, painstakingly drizzles his mornay sauce over everything, then dusts it all with a Cajun spice blend, garnishing with diced parsley.

Patsy waits until the plating is complete before wrapping her arms around Caleb's waist from behind.

"I think you *do* love me," she says, referring to their conversation last night—one he'd thought she wouldn't remember, given her state of inebriation.

"Sit, eat," Caleb says. "Before it gets cold."

Patsy obeys. With just one bite of his Cajun-inspired breakfast, her eyes roll to the back of her head in ecstasy. "Mmm! Your mornay is still the best I ever had."

Caleb smiles. He loves making people happy with his food—women in particular. Especially one as lovely as Patsy, who's wearing just a T-shirt and panties.

He considers, briefly, taking the day off and spending it with her. They could make spicy sweet potato hummus, mix a pitcher of ice-cold juleps, and watch old movies together in bed, just like they used to.

It's an incredibly tempting notion. But Caleb pushes it out of his head.

He's a dedicated homicide detective with a fresh case. And he's wasted enough time already.

After a lingering kiss on the corner of Patsy's lips, Caleb

is out the door before the *Times-Picayune* lands on her welcome mat. Still, he almost immediately finds himself stuck in morning rush-hour traffic. At least that's what he thinks it is. He considers flipping on his police siren, but it looks like a parade of some sort beginning to form on the outskirts of the French Quarter.

Just another day in New Orleans.

"Screw it," Caleb mumbles, and pulls a squealing U-turn.

Instead of inching his way to his office at police headquarters on South Broad Street, he decides to head for the New Orleans coroner's office less than half a mile away.

Rex, the longtime parking attendant, waves hello as Caleb pulls his black Charger past the security gate and into a spot reserved for visiting law enforcement.

"I'm guessing you're not here just to say hello, Detective," Rex says.

"I wish," Caleb says.

Before he gets out, Caleb snatches the crumpled paper bag sitting on the front seat to bring inside with him, filled with jalapeño-raisin biscuits still warm from the oven. He knows Quincy will appreciate them.

He also knows how desperately he's going to need his friend's help.

CHAPTER 9

"WELL, WE WERE RIGHT," the potbellied medical examiner declares as he leads Caleb down the sterile hallway toward his laboratory, his snakeskin boots clicking along the floor. "Official cause of death: poisoning. I'm sure of it. Just as I'm sure these heavenly little biscuits of yours are going to do quite a number on my intestinal tract."

Quincy savors the final flaky bite, then dusts off his fingers and types a code on a keypad affixed above the handle of a large metal door.

"Detective Rooney," Quincy says, as he and Caleb enter the musty lab, "meet Martin Feldman and Elizabeth Keating. You'll forgive them if they're a little quiet this morning."

Laid out side by side on two metal cadaver tables are the male and female victims from Patsy's restaurant. Both are completely naked. Both have long, jagged incisions running from their sternums to their pubic bones.

"Marty and Elizabeth," Caleb repeats solemnly. The two

victims, in his mind, have just been transformed from anonymous corpses into real human beings. His desire to find their killer and avenge their deaths is suddenly intense.

"Unfortunately," Quincy continues, "their names are about the only thing I can tell you for certain. I'm still waiting for the lab results on the tissue samples I sent over. That should give us some idea of what kind of poison was used. I hope."

Caleb is no forensic pathologist but wagers a guess. "Could it be hemlock?"

"That's what I thought, too," Quincy replies, flipping through a messy stack of his handwritten autopsy notes. "Until I sliced open their lungs. Mr. Feldman's had quite a bit of tar buildup. Probably a pack-a-day smoker for years. But there wasn't any of the textbook respiratory system paralysis you'd expect to see."

"What about nightshade?" Caleb asks. "Not common, I know. But it's turned up in a couple homicide cases of mine in the past."

"If they ingested *atropa belladonna,*" Quincy answers, "they would probably have lived long enough for the paramedics to arrive. Might even still be with us."

Caleb thinks. "What about, I don't know…something like strychnine?"

"It has similar symptoms, I'll give you that," Quincy replies. "But it still doesn't quite fit the bill."

"So maybe we're looking at some kind of *man-made* poison. Something new."

"It's possible," Quincy concedes. "Past couple of years, we've been seeing novel strings of synthetic alkaloids and toxins coming out of Chinese labs—stuff that would give whoever was behind Yasser Arafat's death a real run for their money."

He removes his tortoise-shell glasses and shakes his head in pity.

"Whatever it was…these two both died *awful* deaths. The constriction of their airways. The wild spasms of every muscle fiber. The burst blood vessels in their necks and eyes. Whoever slipped 'em their fatal elixir didn't just want 'em to die. They wanted 'em to suffer. Like hell. And they sure as shit did."

Caleb absorbs that for a moment, affected by the pure callousness of the double murder, the killer's cruelty.

But that might also prove to be a critical clue. It could speak to the killer's relationship to the victims—*personal*—and his motive—*revenge*.

Caleb's mind kicks into gear. He tries to retrace his steps last night at Patsy's restaurant, tries to think back to all the people he observed and spoke with.

"Must have been an inside job," he mumbles. It's the only theory that makes sense. But it troubles him, too. It might mean somebody on Patsy's staff committed the murders, and Caleb knows his old flame has a knack for hiring only the very best.

But *that* could mean…Patsy might have done it herself.

No. That's impossible.

Before Caleb can fret any further, he notices Quincy eyeing the grease-stained brown bag he's holding containing those homemade jalapeño-raisin biscuits.

"How about one more for the road, Killer Chef?" Quincy asks with a smile.

Caleb might be feeling frustrated, but he's also feeling generous. He hands his friend the entire sack.

He's got himself a *real* killer to find.

CHAPTER 10

PATSY'S DOESN'T OFFICIALLY OPEN for another ninety minutes, so Caleb wagers that its namesake probably won't show up for at least thirty. Which means he'll have a bit of time to do some investigating on his own before Patsy gets in his hair.

As he parks his Charger in front of the restaurant, Caleb remembers that Mary Ellen Cantrell—a sassy, seventy-something hostess who's worked the busy lunch shift at Patsy's for years—keeps the main entrance dead-bolted until 11:30 a.m. on the dot. She's the type who wouldn't even let her own mother step inside early.

Caleb *could* flash his badge and *make* her open up, of course, but he doesn't want to disrupt or irritate any of the staff more than he has to. So instead he heads around to the back alley and slips in through the kitchen's rear door, finding it propped ajar with an empty wine crate.

"You're back pretty early, Detective."

Helen Broussard, a spunky young prep cook with skin

the color of a New Orleans–style iced coffee with chicory and cream, is mashing and seasoning a small mountain of blanched redskin potatoes.

"I could say the same about you," Caleb replies. Helen was one of the many kitchen employees he spoke with late last night—and here she is the next morning, hard at work.

"The only people in this town with worse hours than cops are chefs," she quips.

"Great," Caleb says. "I'm both. How's the staff holding up?"

"Hangin' in, I suppose," Helen answers. "Most of us are just trying to keep our heads down and make the very best food we can. You know what I'm saying?"

Caleb certainly does.

As he moves through the kitchen, where the mood is palpably tense, Caleb nods hello to some of the other prep cooks and dishwashers he remembers speaking to last night. It's a conscious effort to gain trust and put a friendly face on the not-always-so-friendly New Orleans Police Department.

But he's also looking for anything out of the ordinary. The fact is, any one of these folks could be the killer he's after.

Caleb passes briefly through the restaurant's mostly empty main dining room before heading down a hall toward Patsy's office. Since she has a tendency to misplace her keys, Patsy installed a keypad in place of a traditional lock. And Caleb—who used to sometimes sneak into her office to surprise her for a midday romp—still remembers the code. He enters it and steps inside.

He takes a seat at Patsy's messy desk behind her dusty computer monitor. He clicks open EverWatch, the program she uses to record and manage her restaurant's multiple security cameras. Caleb is well aware that an NOPD forensic tech has already copied all the relevant footage onto an external hard drive for detailed examination back at headquarters. But Caleb wants to see it now for himself.

Pulling up numerous split-screen angles at once of both the dining room and kitchen, he decides to start with the moment of Marty and Elizabeth's deaths.

Just as witnesses said, the two victims appeared to begin choking and gasping more or less simultaneously. They clutched their throats in terror. They jerked and shuddered uncontrollably. Even if Quincy hadn't told him that the victims died in excruciating pain, the video makes it obvious. A few diners and waitstaff can be seen hurrying over to the couple's table and trying desperately to help—but they're too late. Turning blue in the face, Marty and Elizabeth suddenly become stiff, then collapse to the ground.

Caleb takes the briefest moment to compose himself after witnessing the disturbing scene, then starts to rewind the footage, working backward.

He watches the couple chatting, intimate and relaxed, while sipping Chardonnay and slurping oysters Rockefeller. The courses before were colorful jambalaya and juicy, perfectly pink Chateaubriand steak, two of Patsy's specialties.

Caleb realizes his mouth is starting to water at the sight of such a feast—despite the knowledge that one of those dishes was probably laced with a synthetic poison.

Referring back to his interview notes, he tries to pay particular attention to the staff members who handled and prepared the couple's food. Unfortunately, that seems to be just about everybody on the payroll.

Laurel Peck, a bubbly twenty-something waitress with a long mane of golden curls, was Marty and Elizabeth's primary server. She took their orders, brought their waters and a few dishes, and checked on them throughout the evening.

Jimmy LeBeauf, another young server with the grit and good looks of the struggling young actor Caleb knows him to be, also waited on the victims, dropping off their first-course plates and refilling their wine glasses.

The bottle of wine itself was delivered and uncorked by Shelby Jemison, Patsy's snooty sommelier, wearing a crisp three-piece suit. And the couple's plates were bussed by longtime busboy Michael Lopez.

In other words, Caleb can't narrow down the suspects one bit.

Inside the kitchen, it all gets even messier. Caleb counts nine different sous-chefs and prep cooks, including Patsy herself, who helped prepare or plate one or more elements of Marty and Elizabeth's lavish dinner.

Despite his careful scrutiny, Caleb doesn't spot anything obviously fishy. No one palming a tiny vial or sprinkling a plate with a funny-looking "spice." The detective's only hope is that the digital forensic team, who will be combing through the footage in closer detail, might catch something he missed.

Until then, Caleb decides to speak with the two main servers again. It's as good a place to start as any.

CHAPTER 11

CALEB REENTERS THE main dining room, which has a few more staff members buzzing around inside now, preparing for the lunchtime rush. He spots Mary Ellen wiping down a stack of menus at the hostess station.

"Hi there, Mary Ellen. I don't think I saw you last night, did I?"

"No, sir," she answers. "I'd been off for a few hours already. It was date night with my hunk of a husband." She peers over her glasses at him and subtly pushes her ample cleavage together. "By the time all this hell broke loose, we were sitting in our Jacuzzi, sipping champagne—"

"All right then," Caleb says, cutting the older woman off before she shares any more unnecessary details about her sex life. "You seen Jimmy or Laurel around?"

Mary Ellen nods to a booth on the other side of the dining room. Laurel and Jimmy are seated together, but they aren't talking. She's folding cloth napkins; he's refilling salt shakers with a small green funnel.

Both look haunted.

"Morning, guys," Caleb says soberly, sliding a chair up to the booth and sitting in it backward.

The two young servers barely mumble a response. They're clearly still shaken from yesterday's events and their up-close and personal role in it all.

"Listen," Caleb continues. "I won't pretend to know how y'all are feeling. But I won't sugarcoat the facts, either. Like I said last night, one of you could have served Mr. Feldman and Ms. Keating the food or drink that killed them. If you can think of anything you didn't already tell me, anything unusual you saw, anything out of the ordinary—"

"How could this happen?" Laurel suddenly exclaims. "They were just two nice, ordinary people! Who could do a thing like that?" She stops folding the thick napkin in her hands and dabs her eyes with it.

Jimmy the actor does a better job of hiding his emotions, but the shock is clearly still raw for him, too.

"I left Los Angeles and came back here because that city was nuts," he says. "Too unpredictable and dangerous. And now *this* happens. I still can't believe it."

Caleb studies the handsome young man for a moment. Is he hiding something? Or is Caleb—not usually the jealous type—just the tiniest bit envious of Jimmy's youth and good looks? Not that he'd ever show it, of course. But his own advancing age, the occasional gray hair, the inevitable march of time—Caleb thinks about these things more than he'd like to admit. He glances at the salt shakers lined up on the table, each with a few grains of rice at the bottom to help soak up moisture and keep the contents fresh. Caleb wishes such a thing existed for human beings.

"What about the couple themselves, then?" he asks. "Did they say anything unusual? Did you recognize them?"

"I'd waited on them before, yeah," says Jimmy. "Only, like, once or twice. She knew her way around the menu and liked to order for them. He didn't seem to mind. They seemed a little boring, to tell you the truth. But totally normal."

Sensing he won't get much more out of this interview, Caleb stands.

"Thanks for your time. I gave y'all my card last night. Call right away if you think of anything, no matter how small or insignificant it might seem. Okay?"

The two servers nod. Caleb starts to head off—when Laurel gets an idea.

"Detective, do you think it might be…I don't know, a competitor?"

"A competitor?"

"Yeah. Maybe somebody's out to get Patsy. Put us out of business. Maybe it had nothing to do with that couple at all. They were just…wrong place, wrong time. Plenty of people in the Quarter must be jealous of Patsy's success, right?"

"Big difference between jealousy and murder," says JD, the restaurant's head chef. He's walking toward the booth carrying two cups of coffee and has overheard the tail end of the conversation. He hands Caleb one of the steaming mugs. "Ain't that right, Detective?"

"Of course," Caleb says, taking the beverage gratefully and blowing on the surface of the thick, almost velvety-smooth cappuccino. "But right now, it's no worse a theory than any other. Nothing's off the table."

But JD isn't satisfied. "*'Competitor,'*" he says, shaking his head. "Hell, *you're* one of our competitors, Killer Chef. Marlene, too. Ever think about that?"

His ex-wife and business partner a murderer? No, that hasn't exactly crossed Caleb's mind. But he hears, loud and clear, the point JD is trying to make.

"Does Patsy have any enemies?" he asks. "And I don't mean angry food bloggers. *Real* ones, who might want to do this establishment—or her—actual harm."

"She ain't exactly best friends with PETA," JD says. "We get about two pieces of hate mail from them a week."

"PETA? The animal rights group?"

"We do serve an awful lot of meat," says Laurel quietly.

But Caleb dismisses that idea fast. If it were only theft or vandalism, maybe he'd believe it. But Marty and Elizabeth were murdered. Worse, they *suffered*. That's what keeps gnawing at him.

"I gotta get back to the ovens," JD says, walking away. "Be in touch, Detective."

Caleb takes a sip of his coffee and surveys the quiet dining room. Eventually his gaze falls on fateful table 24. A clean white tablecloth has been draped over it, and a small bouquet of flowers rests on top. But otherwise it's bare. No place settings have been laid out. The chairs Marty and Elizabeth sat in are leaned against it at an angle, out of respect.

"You were right about not seating that table for a while, Detective Rooney."

Caleb turns to see Patsy standing beside him. She's wearing a dark pink sundress. Her hair, wet from a recent shower, is pulled back in a ponytail.

"I wasn't quite thinking straight last night," she says. "I'm sorry."

Caleb isn't sure if she means at the restaurant or back in her apartment, or both. Regardless, he answers with a gentle squeeze of her hand.

"This kind of thing shouldn't happen to people like you," he says. "You're *good* people."

Patsy leans into Caleb, and against his better professional judgment he slips an arm around her shoulders and pulls her into a half-hug.

"Then again," Patsy says, "it looks like we sure could use those two seats."

Caleb follows her line of sight to the front of her restaurant. On the sidewalk outside, reporters and would-be diners alike have already gathered. It's an even larger crowd than on a typical weekday afternoon.

Part of Caleb is relieved. His worry that Patsy's business might suffer was clearly unfounded. Of course, he didn't expect her business to actually *increase*. New Orleanians sure do love the grim and macabre.

"Good luck today, Patz," he says, walking back toward the kitchen to slip out the back entrance again. "We'll talk later, all right?"

Caleb takes a final look at table 24 as he passes it. Its stark emptiness reflects how little he knows about the couple that last sat there.

CHAPTER 12

CALEB HAS SCARCELY stepped foot back out into the alleyway when he decides to rectify that situation.

He fires off a text to Janine Newby, his department's hardworking office administrator, asking her to send him the victim dossiers on Martin Feldman and Elizabeth Keating. He knows Janine and a pair of junior homicide detectives worked late into the night compiling them, per standard department procedure.

Within seconds, Caleb's phone buzzes with a new e-mail. He opens it and downloads the attached file, which contains a trove of public and private information on the two victims.

The late couple had apparently been seeing each other for quite some time, even though Marty's divorce from his first wife, Andrea, had been finalized only two months earlier.

Bam! Caleb thinks, clenching his fist in excitement. *A real suspect; a real motive!*

Andrea Feldman's address is listed in the dossier as well.

To Caleb's pleasant surprise, it's not far, but it also isn't what he might have expected. Marty was a modestly successful architect, but his ex lives on a stretch of Esplanade Avenue known as Millionaires' Row, one of the wealthiest and most exclusive sections in all of New Orleans.

Caleb pulls a jalapeño from his pocket and snaps it between his teeth, savoring its familiar zing. This case just got a lot more interesting.

As he cruises past dazzling three-story town houses and elegant Creole mansions, Caleb's mind is already on overdrive. The jealous, murderous ex-wife is one of the oldest clichés there is, but for good reason: they're more common than many realize. If Andrea really was behind the deaths of Marty and Elizabeth—her cheating husband and his home-wrecking mistress—it makes perfect sense that she'd want them both to suffer horrendously. And she obviously has the resources to make it happen.

A woman who must be Andrea is sitting on the second-floor wraparound balcony of her majestic, indigo-colored home when Caleb pulls up. She's engrossed in a leather-bound book, taking a final deep drag on a fragrant clove cigarette.

Caleb makes eye contact and waves. "Hello—Mrs. Feldman?"

With an audible, melancholy sigh, she shuts the book and heads downstairs to let him in.

Andrea opens the door, and Caleb is surprised by her attractiveness. A brunette bombshell with high cheekbones and deep-set hazel eyes, she's lithe but looks tough.

"Mrs. Feldman? I'm Detective Rooney, New Orleans PD." Caleb flashes her his star-and-crescent badge, but Andrea has already turned and gestured for him to enter.

"Let me guess," she says drily. "You're here to talk about a couple of unpaid parking tickets?"

She leads Caleb through her sprawling home's wide central corridor. A series of framed Impressionist paintings of ballerinas line the walls.

"Edgar Degas stayed on Esplanade Avenue when he visited New Orleans," Andrea says, as if it's only natural, therefore, that some of the master's priceless pieces would now be hanging inside her home. She notices him looking. "Are you a fan of his dancers?"

Caleb doesn't quite know what she's talking about, but he answers as honestly as he can without seeming like a total dunce. "I think these ones are all right."

Andrea smirks, leading him into the kitchen, which is unusually spacious and airy given her old home's style. The design and cabinetry are vintage, but the appliances are all stainless steel professional-grade. *This* is the kind of display of wealth that impresses a chef like Caleb—and makes him just a little envious.

"I'll tell you anything you want to know about my ex-husband," Andrea says, pouring steaming water for a fresh pot of black tea. "I read about his death this morning in the paper. I was stunned. But I won't lie to you, Detective. I wasn't sad."

CHAPTER 13

ANDREA BEGINS THE STORY of her marriage to the late Martin Feldman. When they first met, well over a decade ago, they fell madly in love. She had a trust fund, thanks to her great-grandfather—one of New Orleans' most notorious bootleggers—and supported Marty as he finished graduate school and began a career as an architect.

"But it was the usual story—over time we grew apart," Andrea says. "It really came to a head about three years ago. That was when the...*sexual* side of our relationship all but disappeared. Our flame was completely snuffed out. Marty said he'd grown 'bored.' He wanted to do things, *try* things, that I simply didn't have the desire for. Or the *stomach* for."

Caleb watches Andrea pour the tea into two antique Oriental cups. Eyeing this woman's toned, slender body and cascade of shimmering hair, he wonders what kind of man could ever get bored with such a stunning creature for a wife.

Andrea hands Caleb the scalding beverage. He takes

it and blows on it gently—but is careful not to sip. He doesn't want to come off as rude. But he doesn't want to swallow one single drop of *anything* served to him by a woman who may know a thing or two about undetectable poison.

"Before long, Marty met Elizabeth," Andrea continues. "She worked for one of his firm's corporate clients. They seemed happy together. And I was pleased for my husband. That may be difficult to understand, but it's the truth. Of course, I knew our marriage had run its course. The divorce took a while, with so many assets to split, but it was amicable."

In addition to her family's old money, she had become a highly successful novelist in her own right. Publishing under the pen name Juliet Benoit, Andrea is the author of a string of bestselling historical thrillers set in New Orleans during the Civil War. Caleb doesn't read much fiction but recognizes the name from the shelves of bookstores, drugstores, even gas stations all across the city.

The more Caleb listens to Andrea, the more he finds himself drawn to her. She's beautiful, yes, but also has a reserve and vulnerability, as well as an obvious intelligence that only enhances her appeal.

He struggles to keep his attraction from clouding his judgment. Part of him wishes they were sharing a bottle of Malbec at a bistro in the Lower Garden District instead of discussing the life and death of her ex-husband—a crime for which Andrea is still his number-one suspect.

"Did your ex-husband have any enemies that you were aware of, Andrea?"

"Hmm. Well, Marty was a strong personality. As I said, we'd grown apart, and that included keeping our funds separate, so I don't know how his business was doing—he was self-employed as an architect. I know that he often took on projects with the city, and that his interactions with contractors could be a little…fraught. But we didn't have daily cocktail hours to discuss his work."

Finally, Caleb asks point-blank, "So who do you think killed him?"

"I honestly don't have a clue," Andrea replies. "We'd barely spoken in months, since deciding to divorce, except through our lawyers."

"What about last night? Where were you when the murders happened?"

The corners of Andrea's mouth curl into a tiny smile at the idea that he might actually consider *her* somehow involved in Marty and Elizabeth's deaths.

"On a date," she says. "At the opera. Opening night performance of Strauss's *Die Fledermaus*. A Tulane anthropology professor invited me. I'm more of a Verdi girl myself, but it was a pleasant enough evening. Here, have a look for yourself."

Andrea fumbles through her velvet purse until she finds and hands Caleb a torn ticket stub from last night's performance. She shows him a picture on her iPhone to further confirm her alibi: she and the geeky professor posing on the opera house steps, both dressed to the nines.

"See? I'm not big on photos, but Robert insisted. And I sure am glad he did!"

"He's your boyfriend?" Caleb asked.

"No—it was our first date. He's a nice man, but I don't think I'll be seeing him again. There wasn't much of…a *spark*."

From the way she says it, and her gaze, Caleb has a feeling that her thoughts aren't on Marty.

Wishing they had met under different circumstances, he simply hands her his card—pleased that she seems to have a solid alibi, but annoyed that he's reached yet another dead end.

"If you think of anything else, Mrs. Feldman, please give me a ring."

Andrea twirls the card in her fingers. "Can I still call you even if I don't?"

Caleb sets down his untouched cup of tea. "Thank you for your time, ma'am."

Walking past the series of Degas paintings again on his way to the front door, Caleb can't help but think what it might be like to be with a woman like Andrea, someone wealthy and sophisticated. She could teach him about art, opera, literature—all the finer things in life he never knew he wanted.

Before getting back into his Charger, Caleb takes out another crisp jalapeño and pops it into his mouth. Eighteen hours into the case and he's still at the starting line.

And if he didn't get back to the truck soon, Marlene would make sure he was the next body found.

CHAPTER 14

LAISSEZ LES BONS temps rouler. "Let the good times roll!"

Plastered on T-shirts, bumper stickers, shot glasses, even baby onesies up and down Bourbon Street, that unofficial motto perfectly captures the city's contradictory spirit, Caleb thinks. Joyous and indulgent, yet gritty and tenacious.

It's been four days since Martin Feldman and Elizabeth Keating were murdered in cold blood, and the good times have certainly kept on rolling all across the French Quarter and beyond.

The lurid story of the double homicide has slipped from the headlines. The reporters and rubberneckers camped out in front of Patsy's have gone home. Business at the restaurant has settled back to its former levels. Even the bouquet of flowers on table 24 has been removed, and hungry diners are once again being seated there, most of them none the wiser.

Caleb is running down every possible lead.

Quincy has informed him that the lab tests conducted on the victims' food and tissue samples were inconclusive. Traces of an advanced, fatal synthetic alkaloid were indeed discovered in Marty and Elizabeth's bloodstreams. Shockingly, the chemical was also found in *multiple* dishes the couple was eating, including the jambalaya and oysters, which were prepared and handled by completely different staff.

NOPD digital forensic experts have combed through hours of Patsy's security footage from that night, frame by frame. But they've been unable to spot anyone tampering with the victims' food.

Intrigued by Andrea but still suspicious, Caleb assigned a pair of junior detectives to verify her opera alibi. It checked out completely. He also requested they look into her story that she and Marty separated on good terms and hadn't recently been in touch. Those claims, too, seem accurate.

As if Caleb didn't have enough to deal with at his day job, he's also had to pull some extra shifts at Killer Chef— all by himself.

The day after he left her alone on that particularly busy night to race over to Patsy's, Marlene came down with a nasty stomach bug, which of course she blamed on her ex-husband's "selfish" behavior. With his partner in culinary crime still laid up in bed, it's fallen on Caleb alone to keep their famous sandwiches coming and their demanding customers happy.

Which is where the detective is now—working the 9:00 p.m. to midnight shift. The truck is parked on Rampart Street on the outskirts of Louis Armstrong Park. Despite some light drizzle, the line is around the block.

Inside this sweltering metal box, Caleb is racing back and forth, sweating like a pig. He's taking orders, throwing money around, slapping sandwiches together like a madman, popping jalapeños like an addict.

But he is completely in his element, one hundred percent in the zone. He's staying calm and focused—still managing to flirt with his female customers with professional charm.

Caleb hands a pair of Hob-Gobblers—slices of hickory-smoked turkey breast slathered with habanero marmalade—to two drunk, platinum-blond older women. He winks at them, making the cougars giggle like schoolgirls. One even slips him a paper napkin with HOTEL MONTELEONE ROOM 217 written on it in ruby-red lipstick.

But before Caleb can even entertain the offer, he feels his cell phone buzz in his back pocket and hears Céline Dion's sappy "The Power of Love" start to play.

"Damnit, Marlene!" he exclaims with a laugh and a resigned shake of his head. She must have changed his ringtone again last night. Nice way to repay his kindness in bringing over some Cajun-style spicy chicken soup.

Caleb ignores the call and redoubles his sandwich-making efforts, but his cell rings a second time. Again he simply ignores it. But then it rings a *third* time.

Caleb is starting to get a bad feeling deep inside his gut. He rips off the sanitary latex gloves he's wearing and pulls out his phone.

The three missed calls all came from Janine back at the station. She answers on the first ring.

"Sorry, Caleb," she says. "Got some bad news. I know you're working tonight. But a sergeant on scene wants you *working* tonight."

He knows exactly what that means: a fresh dead body has just been discovered, a fresh case has been born, and for some reason, it involves *him*. As if he didn't have his hands full already.

"Well, shit, Janine," Caleb huffs. "Why can't one of the other Ds take it instead?" Caleb is proud to be among the NOPD's finest homicide detectives, but he's certainly not the only one.

Janine exhales deeply before answering.

"He thinks you're going to want to see this."

CHAPTER 15

"SORRY, FOLKS, WE'RE closin' early!"

A chorus of boos and groans erupts from the line of waiting customers as Caleb starts hastily shutting down his truck. He latches the outside service windows. Flips off the deep fryer. Powers down the electric griddle. Padlocks the cash register.

He hates that he has to shutter his business like this—and *dreads* the tongue-lashing he's going to get tomorrow from Marlene. But duty calls.

Because Caleb started making sandwiches right after his police shift ended that day, he still has his badge and service weapon clipped to his belt. But instead of a collared shirt, tie, and dress shoes, he's wearing a grease-stained wifebeater and an old pair of rubber chef's clogs.

Oh, well, he thinks, locking the truck's rear door and hurrying down St. Philip Street on foot. The French Quarter is so swarmed on this hot, drizzly summer night with tourists and locals, bikers, and horse-drawn carriages, that even with his siren blaring it would take longer to drive the half-mile to his destination than simply jog there.

Caleb soon reaches it: Café Du Monde, the legendary open-air coffee shop on Decatur Street, nestled right along the banks of the Mississippi. It's the location of his and Marlene's first date all those years ago.

Now it's the backdrop for a heinous crime.

Caleb notes the scrum of emergency vehicles and police officers blocking off the building from the boisterous crowds and gathering paparazzi. He shows his badge to a young officer standing at the scene's perimeter. The cop raises an eyebrow at the detective's odd attire but lifts up the yellow police tape to let him pass.

Caleb is instantly struck with an eerie sense of déjà vu. Just like a few nights ago at Patsy's, he sees clusters of shaken patrons speaking with police officers, who are preventing witnesses from leaving.

And at a table over in the corner, strewn with knocked-over cups of coffee and a plate of half-eaten beignets, a forensic investigator is snapping pictures.

Of a well-dressed man and woman splayed out on the ground.

Both dead.

Caleb steps closer. The two victims look to be around the same age and same professional "type" as Marty and Elizabeth. The man is a bit stocky, white, and the woman appears to be at least part Asian. Their bodies are twisted in similarly unnatural poses. And their faces are frozen in almost identical masks of pain.

It takes Caleb all of six milliseconds to deduce that the two double murders are connected. Similar victims, similar MO, similar location. Could this be another crime of passion? A copycat attack? Or the beginning of a terrifying pattern?

Sergeant Roy Jardell—dedicated, but plenty cynical after nineteen long years on the force—approaches Caleb.

"Four bodies in four days. Unbelievable, ain't it? Nice outfit by the way, Detective. You look like Emeril Lagasse on steroids."

Caleb ignores the little dig. "Thanks for the call, Roy," he says. "When Janine gave me the briefing I hoped—prayed—it was just a coincidence. Another couple killed while they ate. But clearly this case just got more complicated."

"According to their IDs," Jardell says, referring to his notepad, "their names are Brent Grassley and Joanna Fujimoto. Both local. An insurance adjuster and a dental hygienist. Friends? Lovers? We're still trying to work that out.

"My team are taking down witness statements and personal details from everyone who was at the coffee shop. They're searching the scene for any additional clues. And they're securing surveillance footage."

Caleb decides *not* to tell Jardell that that's exactly what his team did after the killings at Patsy's—and it was all a total wash.

"We also got the press up our asses on this one," Jardell says with a frown. "What a pack of vultures. Rumors are already flying that the four murders are related. Want to release any kind of statement?"

Caleb feels a flicker of pleasure imagining how Tariq—that smug little pipsqueak from the mayor's office—might literally have a heart attack if the New Orleans Police Department announced that a cold-blooded serial killer was stalking the French Quarter, murdering innocent couples. But he thinks better of it.

"Not yet," Caleb answers. "Not till we know more. No reason to get everybody all riled up for no reason."

Caleb reaches into his pocket for a jalapeño—and is dismayed to discover that his trusty plastic bag is empty.

It's a shockingly uncomfortable feeling, like a drinker discovering his bottle has only dregs, or a smoker reaching the end of his pack.

Caleb hopes it's not a bad omen. But in this city of voodoo and witchcraft, it just might be.

CHAPTER 16

"I THINK I NEED a little air," says Caleb to Sergeant Jardell.

Café Du Monde is *open*-air, but neither says so. It's just that kind of evening.

A whole lot of things go unspoken.

Caleb steps out from under the giant green canopy and onto the café's empty side patio. The noise and chaos of the street are still close by, but at least he has a bit of privacy here to clear his head, to gather his thoughts.

Quincy and his team are on their way over to bag the two new bodies and run tests on their food and coffee. But Caleb already has a feeling what they'll find: not much. Some similar traces of the same synthetic alkaloid that poisoned Marty and Elizabeth, sure. But nothing that will actually help them track down who's responsible.

Meanwhile, forensic specialists will dust for prints and fibers, and comb through every frame of the café's security footage. Caleb is hopeful they'll catch a break that way. But his gut is telling him they won't.

The fact is, they're obviously dealing with someone smart. Someone cruel. Someone who knows how to hide their tracks. Someone with a specific agenda and vendetta…against couples on a date? Against diners enjoying a meal?

Caleb mentally runs through all the facts again. They just don't make any sense. The killer doesn't fit any profile, doesn't match any—

"Hey, I know you!"

The perky female voice comes from Caleb's left. He looks over to see a pretty, thirty-something redhead in a professional blouse and pencil skirt leaning against the police barricade, clutching a microphone.

"Nah, I don't think so," Caleb mumbles, turning back to face the café.

He does know her, as a cute local reporter for the WVUE-TV evening news. She's also a spunky, flirty weekend regular at his food truck—usually a few sheets to the wind when she orders, yet always asks for light spicy mayo on her shrimp po' boy and an extra pickle. On more than one occasion, she's also asked for Caleb's number.

"Yeah," she insists, "you're Killer Chef! You catch bad guys *and* make the best sandwiches in town."

"Thanks," Caleb says, trying to cut her off.

"Got those eating jalapeños in your pocket? I've seen you. I bet you're carrying some right now, aren't you?"

"Actually, I just ran out," Caleb says. "Listen, I gotta head back inside."

"Wait, wait one second," she says. A cameraman has appeared behind her and is starting to roll. "What can you tell us about what happened here, Detective? My sources say you're running the investigation. Do you have any additional insight, since you're part of the New Orleans food scene yourself?"

"No comment," Caleb says gruffly. He's not in any mood to talk to the press or become part of the story himself.

He starts heading back into the café. But that doesn't stop the cute reporter from shouting more questions at him.

"Are tonight's murders connected to the double homicide earlier this week at Patsy's?" she calls out. "Do you have a description of the suspect yet? What would you say to all the tourists and local residents who are too afraid to eat out?"

Caleb smirks a bit at that last question—thinking about the line for the truck that night—until he sees Quincy and his assistants zipping up Brent and Joanna's body bags. His smile disappears. He and Quincy exchange a grim nod.

Caleb enters the men's room. He knows there's a chance the killer might have slipped inside to change clothes, don a disguise, or flush some evidence, so Caleb is careful not to touch anything. The entire place will soon be processed by crime scene techs, floor to ceiling.

God, his head is throbbing. Caleb uses a latex glove to gently turn on a tap and splash a little cold water on his face. In the mirror in the bathroom's harsh fluorescent light, he notices small bags under his eyes and crow's-feet in the corners. His complexion looks pale, almost ghostly.

Caleb exits the restroom and looks around the café at all the officers interviewing patrons, the forensic technicians getting to work.

Realistically, there's nothing more for him to do here tonight. After such a long day, he decides to head home and get some rest. He wants to be fresh and alert to tackle the case tomorrow.

Ducking back under the crime scene tape into the hot, rainy night and walking up the sidewalk the way he came, Caleb feels his cell phone buzz. Next comes that damn Céline Dion ringtone again.

He checks the caller ID: MARLENE.

Against his better judgment—and hoping he can keep the early closing of the food truck a secret at least until tomorrow—he answers.

"Hey, Mar. I can't really talk right now. But how are you feeling? Better?"

"Well, aren't you just sweet as king cake," she replies, her voice dripping with her usual sarcasm. "How are *you* feeling, Caleb? I know how exhausting it is making all those sandwiches by yourself. The line's gotta be down the block tonight. How's it going?"

"Uh…pretty good," he answers, stepping around a drunk college student puking a stream of Hurricane-blue vomit into a gutter. "Busy. But nothing I can't handle."

"Oh, you're so full of it!" Marlene snaps. "Here I am, sick in bed, when all of a sudden I see your big ol' mug pop up on the evening news—at a crime scene! Some red-headed reporter was giving your whole life story. You know what the bottom of the screen said? *'Killer Chef Lead Detective on Foodie Murders.'* Congratulations, Caleb. You did it. You're famous. For all the wrong reasons."

Caleb sighs in frustration. *Great.* For years he'd worked hard to keep his two very different professional lives separate. But now, they've come together. In the worst possible way.

And with the whole city watching him, he knows things can get even worse.

CHAPTER 17

LESS THAN TWENTY-FOUR hours later, Caleb is right back where he started—inside the hot-as-hell Killer Chef truck.

While he slathers a sliced roll with horseradish-infused mustard and pops a fresh jalapeño into his mouth from his refilled bag, Marlene is rummaging through the produce bins in their truck's mini-refrigerator.

"Is this really all the sweet onions we have left?" she asks, clearly irritated. "We're almost out of tomatoes. Bell peppers, too. Nice going yesterday, man."

"Sorry," Caleb says with an eye roll. "I didn't get a chance to do inventory last night. I was a little busy. Trying to solve four murders and all."

Marlene stifles a cough in the crook of her elbow. Because Caleb shut the truck down early yesterday—which cost them a few hundred dollars in lost sales—she insisted they pull a double shift today: lunch *and* dinner. With her partner tied up most of the morning and afternoon with the case, Marlene guzzled about a gallon of DayQuil and dragged her sick self to work.

"Well, you better solve 'em fast, bud," she says, dabbing her sweaty brow. "Our business is in the gutter thanks to you. It's down all across the French Quarter."

She's right. After his handsome face was plastered all over the news last night, Caleb and Marlene both hoped the newfound notoriety might boost their food truck's sales. Instead, their line of customers is only a fraction of the usual—which is why, instead of slaving nonstop over the stove and fryer, Marlene has time to go through the fridge. And bust Caleb's balls.

"Don't you dare put this on *me*," Caleb says. "After what's been happening this week, can you really blame people for deciding to eat at home?"

Marlene shuts the refrigerator, opens the truck's rear door, and sits down on the bumper. "I even wore my running shoes today and everything," she says, gesturing to her pair of hot-pink kicks. She lights up a Virginia Slim and sucks in a long drag. "If things don't pick up, I might take a *real* break and go in for a tarot reading, see if my future looks any brighter than my present."

Caleb smiles at this idea and recalls a fond memory.

"Remember the first time you got your cards read?" he asks.

"Of course I do. It was our first day of school. And we went together."

Years ago, when she had just moved to New Orleans and

Caleb was still a rookie beat cop, they found themselves at side-by-side stovetops in the same Introduction to French Sauces course. During the initial get-to-know-each-other portion of the class, Marlene confessed a desire to have her cards read. That very night, Caleb offered to take her.

"Remember what that kooky old broad said?" Marlene asks.

Caleb most definitely does.

As he and Marlene sat together in the psychic's dark, cramped parlor watching her flip over card after colorful card, the woman told them that they would someday get hitched.

"I thought she probably said that to *every* young girl who came in there with a hunky guy," Marlene says, "just so she'd get a bigger tip."

"Same here," answers Caleb, "until she flipped over the next batch of cards and told us, 'You will remain life partners, yet will suffer great hardship.'"

Sure enough, the old Gypsy was right.

Just a few months after they met, Marlene became pregnant. She and Caleb held a classic shotgun wedding, a small picnic for family and their closest friends under the moss-draped oak trees of City Park.

At first, their marriage was strong and loving. Marlene suffered a miscarriage—yet it only brought them closer. But then it happened again. Then again.

When it became clear that children weren't in their future, the two decided to have a different kind of "baby." They opened up their first joint eatery, a crêpe stand, not far from where they tied the knot.

But the place didn't last. And neither did their marriage. They still loved each other, but more like siblings than husband and wife.

On their seventh wedding anniversary, they held a spectacular rabbit and sausage jambalaya dinner for all their friends. During dessert—homemade pralines and coffee with cream and chicory—they announced they'd amicably filed for divorce that very morning, and offered a toast to their continued friendship.

"At least we got one hell of a party out of it," Marlene muses.

"Yeah, I'd say we made out all right," Caleb responds, putting the final touches on the smoked ham sandwich he's been making and wrapping it in wax paper. "Hey, hand me a pickle, would you?"

But Marlene doesn't answer. Caleb glances over at her. She's holding her cigarette near her lips, mid-drag. Something's caught her attention off in the distance.

And she looks concerned.

"What's up, Mar? What are you looking at?"

Marlene tosses her cigarette butt to the ground.

"Hurry up and finish that sandwich, Caleb. I think we might have a little trouble."

CHAPTER 18

CALEB HASTILY HANDS the sandwich to the waiting customer and then follows Marlene's nod. Across the street, a dark figure wearing a blue hooded sweatshirt is leaning against a lamppost, staring right at them—then nervously glances away.

"Guy's been there a while," Marlene says, mashing her cigarette with the toe of her running shoe. "Noticed him about half an hour ago. I thought he looked a little odd, but I didn't think much of it. New Orleans has its fair share of weirdos, after all. But then when I realized he was still there…"

"Maybe he's just waiting for somebody," says Caleb, watching the man futzing with his iPhone. "Maybe he's playing a game."

"Look closer," Marlene says. The mystery man holds up his phone as if taking a picture. "He's filming us or something. And he sure doesn't look like a food blogger."

Caleb furrows his brow. Marlene's right. Something

feels a little off about this fellow, a little unsettling. So Caleb unties his apron and goes to the truck's exit.

He's barely stepped into the street when the man suddenly turns and dashes off.

"Hey, wait!" Caleb shouts, but the stranger doesn't slow. He hooks a left onto Dumaine Street and disappears into a crowd.

And the chase is on.

Caleb picks up speed and tries to keep up. He watches the man turn onto Bourbon Street, which—despite the recent murders in the area—seems as packed and chaotic as ever.

"Police, out of the way!" Caleb yells, pushing tourists aside as he barrels along.

But the mystery man still stays a few steps ahead.

After passing St. Ann Street, the man ducks into Marie Laveau's House of Voodoo, a squat wood-paneled museum and souvenir shop dedicated to one of New Orleans' most notorious spiritual practices.

Caleb bursts inside after him.

The tiny shop is packed to the gills with voodoo masks, colorful gems, and tiny felt astrology bags. Caleb pauses briefly, looks around…and sees the man shove a screaming patron out of his way and rush through the rear door.

Caleb chases after him—bumping into a giant crystal ball that falls to the floor and shatters into a million pieces, prompting furious screams and a string of curses from the woman behind the register.

Next Caleb passes through a dim, disheveled hallway, nearly tripping on a toppled wooden statue and an overturned crate of tarot cards the mystery man had tossed in his path.

Caleb soon reaches the shop's rear exit, which leads to a small, enclosed backyard garden. He now spots the man again—scaling the wall. Caleb jumps up and lunges for the man's ankle, but he misses. He falls to the concrete ground. Hard.

Then looks up to see the man slip over the top of the wall and disappear again.

Damnit!

Caleb is in pain. His ankle is throbbing and he's getting some real bad heartburn from all those jalapeños he's been munching.

But he picks himself up with a grunt. And keeps going.

He exits the garden via a wooden door that leads to the street, just in time to see the man rounding the corner. Caleb pursues, limping now, but not giving up.

"Police!" he calls out again, waving his badge in the air. This time he also adds: "Somebody stop that guy!"

Most of the tourists Caleb passes look bewildered by the request, like deer in headlights. Or maybe it's just from all the booze. Either way, they're of no help—and the mystery man is starting to put more and more distance between Caleb and himself.

But just when he despairs, Caleb encounters some guardian angels. Literally.

Two hulking men in white T-shirts and red berets—members of the New Orleans chapter of the Guardian Angels, a nonprofit citizen patrol group—stop and intervene. They try to grab the man as he races by them. But the runner twists and resists and manages to shake off their grip and keep running.

Still, that brief delay helps.

Caleb finally manages to catch up to the man—and tackles him to the pavement, right in the middle of the street.

"Who...the hell...are you!" Caleb demands, desperately out of breath.

The man is too winded to answer, so as soon as Caleb slaps some cuffs on him, he starts feeling around his pockets for his wallet—or for a weapon.

"I didn't do nothing wrong!" the man pleads, coughing and gasping for air. "What are you arresting me for? This is police brutality, man!"

Caleb locates his wallet and flips it open with one hand, keeping the squirming man pinned down with the other. His driver's license shows a local address and what Caleb considers a rather unusual name: Mitchell Albatross-Gomez, thirty-two years old.

"I'm *not* arresting you, Mr. Albatross-Gomez. At least not yet. You're simply being detained. Wanna tell me why you were filming me back at my truck?"

"I was just taking some pictures, jeez! I know who you are, man, and I'm gonna sue your ass. Look how many witnesses I got!"

Caleb glances around. About a dozen or so tourists and pedestrians have stopped to watch the confrontation, mumbling among themselves with concern. Ironically, but not surprisingly, nearly all are filming the scene with their cell phones.

Caleb needs a police brutality reprimand like he needs a hole in his head. And he knows that his grounds for keeping Mitchell in custody are shaky at best: taking photos or shooting video in a public place, as well as running from an off-duty police officer, aren't crimes.

Caleb is dying to question Mitchell further, but he doesn't want to push his luck. For now, he'll take what he can get.

He's got the guy's name. He can start to do some digging.

"My apologies for the inconvenience, sir," Caleb says with a grimace, uncuffing Mitchell and handing him back his wallet. He even helps the man to his feet—mostly as a gesture of goodwill for all the cameras.

"You cops are all freakin' crazy!" Mitchell barks, dusting

himself off and quickly backing away. "You're a bunch of…of…animals!"

What a weird, creepy nut, Caleb thinks as he watches Mitchell disappear back into the crowd, which quickly begins to dissipate when it's clear the show is over.

What a weird, creepy world.

CHAPTER 19

"I HEARD SOMEONE went for a little jog last night through the French Quarter?"

Dorothy Fiddler greets Caleb at the door to her darkened office. At sixty-six, with a frizzy bob of gray hair and chunky purple reading glasses, she could easily pass as a librarian, or somebody's kindly grandmother.

Instead, she's one of the NOPD's top digital forensic analysts, a total technical badass.

"Funny stuff, Dorothy. You want the usual bribe I got for you or not?"

With a smile she takes one of the two steaming cups of coffee Caleb is holding, as well as the paper bag of freshly baked beignets. Since she's a bit too old and cynical to be charmed by Caleb's flirtations and good looks, he curries favor with her by culinary means. Which works every time.

"Come in and grab a front-row seat, Detective. I've got something to show you."

Dorothy plops down in her desk chair in front of three

giant plasma computer screens. Caleb hovers behind her, bobbing from one foot to the next, partly because his ankle is still hurting from last night, but mostly in anticipation.

Dorothy taps the space bar, and numerous synced-up angles of security camera footage taken both inside and outside Café Du Monde begin to play.

Caleb tries to keep tabs on all the feeds at once, but he focuses primarily on Brent and Joanna sitting together, eating and sipping their coffee in silence.

Then, all of a sudden—though the footage is black and white—it's clear they both start turning blue.

Their eyes bulge. They clutch at their throats and chests. They wave desperately for help. Then they shake, spasm, and collapse. It's another horrible pair of deaths that eerily resemble the ones at Patsy's.

"Well, did you see it?" Dorothy asks, taking a sip of her coffee. Her maroon lipstick leaves a giant imprint on the cup's edge.

"You know I didn't," Caleb answers, growing frustrated. "Show me again."

Dorothy's wrinkled fingers fly across her keyboard. A digital copy of Mitchell Albatross-Gomez's Louisiana driver's license pops up on-screen. So does a booking photo taken a few years ago, in which his hair is a bit longer and scragglier. Next, a flurry of colorful pixels dance across both images, analyzing them.

"I pulled the suspect's DMV photo and old mug shots, like you asked. Then I ran them through our Centurion facial recognition program. Next, I executed a full metadata scan across every frame of—"

"I get it, Dorothy, you're a whole lot smarter than me. Just cut to the chase."

Dorothy smiles as she rewinds all the footage and replays it. A digital yellow halo appears around the face of a young man wearing sunglasses and a Saints cap, sitting alone at a table on the opposite side of the café.

Caleb gasps. "Is that…?"

"It's him, all right," Dorothy replies. "Keep watching."

Again Brent and Joanna start to squirm and shudder. But this time, Caleb notices that Mitchell uses all the commotion as cover—nervously standing, glancing around, then slipping out the side entrance completely unseen.

"I knew it!" Caleb exclaims, clapping Dorothy on the shoulder.

"Unfortunately," she says with disappointment, "I couldn't find a single shot of anybody tampering with their food or drinks. And Albatross-Gomez never comes within twenty feet of the two victims or their table. I also reviewed the footage from Patsy's again, but he wasn't there that night."

Dorothy and Caleb share a look. It's hardly concrete proof that Mitchell is the killer. But it's a start.

"What do we know about the guy?" Dorothy asks.

Caleb mentally runs through the results of the background check he ran on Mitchell earlier that morning. "Not much. He's lived in the bayou most of his life. He's a drifter. A drinker. A user. Did a few months at Dixon for possession, B&E. Nothing violent…but God knows what he's capable of."

Caleb looks back at Dorothy's computer screens. His eyes bore into the back of Mitchell's head as the man nervously flees the scene.

What's his involvement in all this? Caleb wonders. *Is he the brains behind it? Just an accomplice? Or was he simply in the wrong place at the right time?*

Caleb's thoughts are interrupted by the buzz of his cell phone in his back pocket—followed by the peppy intro to Beyoncé's "Single Ladies."

"Sorry, my ex-wife…" Caleb starts to explain to Dorothy, a little embarrassed, but he leaves it at that.

He answers the call, from Janine.

And he nearly drops his phone in shock.

CHAPTER 20

CALEB DOESN'T REMEMBER anything Janine told him after she broke the news.

He doesn't remember racing to his trusty black Charger and speeding across town toward Tulane, siren blaring, almost T-boning a delivery truck along the way.

He doesn't remember storming through the front entrance of one of his favorite restaurants, Clancy's—serving incredible classic Creole dishes since the 1940s—startlingly empty for a midday lunch service.

All Caleb remembers is seeing the bodies.

Another professional-looking couple. The man sprawled on the ground, the woman hunched over the table, her face literally planted in the food that just killed them.

Victims five and six.

This time, murdered in broad daylight.

Caleb speaks briefly with Officer Hal Boulet, the nervous, fresh-faced cop who was the first to respond to the 911 call.

"I tried my damnedest to corral as many witnesses as I could," Boulet says, "but I was on my own. By the time backup arrived, most of 'em had run off. They were terrified. But the owner told me there weren't that many customers here to begin with."

Caleb isn't surprised—that business is down, or that folks freaked out and ran off after another double murder. He reassures the young officer that he did fine. He's not too concerned right now with interviewing people who likely didn't see anything anyway.

"I'm gonna be broadcasting a possible suspect photo and description out to every PMC in a five-mile radius," Caleb says, referring to the Police Mobile Computer system installed inside every cruiser and unmarked car in the department. He's already got his phone out and is texting the request for an all-points bulletin to Janine, who'll make it happen.

"Tell the others I want the scene secured," Caleb continues. "But more important, I want to do a full sweep for this guy. He's a tweaker with a rap sheet who was at Café Du Monde two nights ago when the last couple was killed. Then I saw him outside my food truck. Tried to talk to him but he bolted. If he was here today, too, I want to catch the bastard."

"Yes, sir," Boulet answers, then moves off to share the instructions.

"Caleb…thank God…this is un-friggin'-believable!"

Mikey Balducci, the husky Sicilian general manager of Clancy's whom Caleb has known for years, is lumbering toward him. An affectionate and emotional man on an average day, Mikey is practically trembling. He looks like a total wreck. He wraps Caleb in a bear hug that nearly knocks the detective off his feet.

"I saw the whole thing," Mikey says, wiping away a tear with a finger the size of a sausage link. "They were regulars. Jonah something-or-other. A finance guy. And Charlotte. Taught history at the college. Married. Been comin' in forever. I'd just set down their crawfish étouffée myself. A second later, I looked back and…and they…"

Mikey trails off, overcome by the unspeakable memory.

"It's going to be okay, Mikey," Caleb says. Reaching into his pocket, he grabs a fistful of jalapeños—which he crushes between his fingers in rage. "We're going to get this son of a bitch. I know we will."

Caleb is trying to be comforting—for the sake of the manager, but mostly for himself.

Six vicious murders in as many days, targeting New Orleans' culinary world and upper class.

Un-friggin'-believable is right.

It all feels like a bad dream.

That's just become a nightmare.

CHAPTER 21

NORMALLY, CALEB WOULD BE tingling with excitement if he was waiting to meet a beautiful woman for cocktails at sunset at a romantic outdoor café.

But the past few days have been anything but normal.

The "Grim Waiter"—as the press has sensationally dubbed whoever is poisoning diners while they eat—is still on the prowl.

And Killer Chef is still miles away from making an arrest.

The APB for Mitchell that Caleb ordered after the last two murders at Clancy's was a total wash. No witnesses inside the restaurant remembered seeing him before or after the killings. If Mitchell was there that afternoon, he got out lickety-split. Caleb has ordered an unmarked car to stake out his last known address in the Lower Ninth Ward, just in case the guy shows. But he's not holding his breath.

Otherwise, it's been a frustrating forty-eight hours of false leads and dead ends. Quincy's latest autopsies and lab results yielded nothing Caleb didn't already know. And good old Dorothy, the forensic tech whiz, couldn't work her magic this time: Clancy's ancient security camera system died a few weeks ago and the owners hadn't gotten around to fixing it.

But then Caleb got a message, relayed by Janine.

"Some woman named Andrea," Janine told him. "She didn't give a last name. Says it's urgent and sounded pretty upset. You think it's about the case?"

"That's the ex-wife of Martin Feldman, one of the victim's at Patsy's. Maybe she remembered something."

He called Andrea back immediately. Not just because of the chemistry he'd felt—she was also still very much a person of interest in the case. Whatever she wanted to tell him, he was willing to listen. And he wasn't disappointed. Andrea had something to share—something big, she said—but insisted on meeting in person. Desperate for even the tiniest scrap of new information, Caleb suggested a quiet outdoor café in the Lower Garden District.

"I wasn't sure you'd come," he says as Andrea takes a seat at his table.

She's wearing oversized sunglasses, but Caleb can see that her eyes are puffy and her mascara is smudged, as if she's been crying. Odd. He pretends not to notice.

"It's lovely to see you again, Mrs. Feldman," he adds. "How are you doing?"

"I…I've been…" Andrea stutters and swallows hard. "These past few days…I can't even begin to tell you just how…how terrible I…"

Andrea fumbles to light a clove cigarette but drops her lighter on the glass table with a clank. Caleb picks it up and sparks it for her, then gently touches her arm.

"It's all right. Take your time. You've been through a lot."

The first time Caleb met Andrea at her mansion, she was so cool and collected. She came off as an aloof intellectual, sexy but snooty. Even a little dangerous. She could very well be the Grim Waiter. But now, she seems scared and vulnerable. Somehow, in the glow of the setting sun, Andrea looks even *more* beautiful than ever.

"Thank you, Detective. It's true. Eight days ago I lost my ex-husband. Then six days ago, I…I lost my ex-boyfriend."

Caleb frowns, not sure what she means. She couldn't possibly be referring to…

"Brent Grassley," she says. "That's right. The second man who was poisoned. At Café Du Monde."

Caleb can turn on the charm, but he's a godawful actor. His shock is written all over his face.

"Well, 'boyfriend' might be the wrong word," Andrea concedes. "But we dated quite seriously for the better part of four months. Quite *secretly* as well. Brent is—*was*—still married to Joanna at the time. They were going through a rough patch, but he refused to leave her. We met through some mutual friends. He asked me out for coffee. At Café Du Monde. One thing led to another. For our one-month 'anniversary,' he took me to dinner…at Patsy's. And now…Brent is dead, too."

Andrea chokes back a sob. But Caleb is too stunned to make a sound.

If what she's saying is true, if she really was romantically involved with two of the three male victims poisoned within days of each other…and she admits familiarity with two of the three crime scenes…motive, means, opportunity—she checks all the boxes, and then some.

Andrea is either the unluckiest woman in all of New Orleans, or she might as well sign a complete confession.

"I know what you're thinking, Detective," Andrea says. "After I heard Brent died, I couldn't believe it myself. I knew if I told you about us, you'd be even more suspicious of me than you are already. But I knew if I *didn't* tell you…if you found out yourself…"

Andrea sucks the last bit of life from her cigarette and then snuffs it out.

"And, no," she adds. "The night of Brent's murder, this time I *don't* have an alibi. I poured myself a big glass of Malbec and went to bed early. Alone."

Caleb simply nods, processing everything Andrea has just

told him, trying desperately to make some sense of it all.

He's still extremely attracted to this sharp, sultry woman sitting across from him.

But now he's also a little scared of her.

Which makes her even hotter.

CHAPTER 22

"SURROUND THE HOUSE, fall into position, wait to move on my order. Got it?"

A chorus of "Yes, sir!" echoes throughout the speeding van.

Caleb is seated among a dozen men clad in black fatigues and armed with assault rifles. They're members of the NOPD's Special Operations Division, otherwise known as New Orleans SWAT.

With the sun just inching over the horizon, they're on their way to execute a high-risk search warrant on the suspected Grim Waiter.

Clancy's restaurant may not have had working security cameras the night of the most recent murders. But after crime scene investigators finished combing the place top to bottom, they found a partial fingerprint on a tabletop, probably left days earlier, that belonged to a key suspect.

One Mitchell James Albatross-Gomez.

Caleb finally had enough evidence to convince a mag-

istrate judge to issue an arrest warrant. And after the unmarked unit outside Mitchell's home spotted the guy
stumbling into his building late last night, Caleb called in
the cavalry.

The van rumbles along, its siren off to maximize the element of surprise. Caleb tightens the straps of his Kevlar
vest. He rechecks the clip of his trusty Glock 22. He pops
one final jalapeño into his mouth.

He's ready.

The vehicle rolls up in front of a rundown single-story
home with discolored paint and a sagging foundation—
faint signs of Katrina damage, even after all these years.

Caleb and the others slip out of the van, fan out, and on
his signal, breach.

They cry out, *"Police!" "Search warrant!" "Get on the
ground!"*

Within seconds they've swept through the entire
crummy place. It's Caleb who actually finds Mitchell—
cowering in the hall closet, wearing nothing but a pair of
stained white boxer shorts.

Mitchell screams in shock but, wisely, doesn't try to run
away or resist arrest this time. He surrenders and lets himself be put in handcuffs.

As an officer reads him his Miranda rights and leads
him outside, Caleb and the others begin the search of his
cluttered, filthy little shack.

It's a total hellhole. Dirty plates are stacked high in the sink. Flies buzz around an overflowing garbage can. Empty liquor bottles and drug paraphernalia—singed spoons, used syringes—are strewn around the bedroom. A loaded .22 revolver, its serial number illegally scratched off, is sitting on top of the dresser.

In addition to six murders, they now have plenty else to charge Mitchell with.

"Detective Rooney? You gotta see this."

Sergeant Dion Chu, a muscular SWAT team leader with a shaved head as shiny as wet ice, beckons Caleb into the living room.

Pinned on the wall is a map of New Orleans. Sure enough, the three crime scenes are marked.

Mitchell's laptop is open on the table. A quick glance at the browser shows an array of news bits about the murders.

Most chilling of all are the photographs on the table: each of the six victims…and one of Caleb and Marlene inside the Killer Chef truck. It's one haunting collage….

But it fills Caleb with grim satisfaction. They caught the bastard!

CHAPTER 23

CALEB LIKES TO KEEP his suspects waiting. He likes to watch them squirm.

A lot of cops don't. They feel the more time a suspect or witness has to mentally prepare his story, the more evasive he'll be during questioning. But Caleb's years of experience have taught him otherwise. Let criminals stew a bit, let them sweat, and they'll be more likely to contradict themselves—and, Caleb hopes, confess.

"Mr. Albatross-Gomez," he says, finally entering the sterile interrogation room after letting Mitchell sit in there alone for forty minutes. He sits down at the metal table across from him. "We meet again."

Mitchell's eyes are darting all over. His breathing is quick and shallow. The room is air-conditioned but his brow is damp. All classic signs of withdrawal—or guilt.

"Whatever you think I did," Mitchell whispers, shaking his head, "I...I didn't."

"You weren't at the scenes of all six murders? You didn't have pictures of them? You didn't kill all those people?"

Mitchell shuts his eyes tight and starts rocking back and forth. The guy is clearly unbalanced.

"I…I was there," Mitchell admits. "And…yeah, I did. But I didn't kill anybody, I swear! I was just the—the delivery guy, you know?"

"No. I don't. Explain it to me."

"There were these little cardboard boxes. Okay? All I did was drop them off at the restaurants. I got paid a thousand bucks each time. That's a fortune to me, man!"

"'Little cardboard boxes,'" Caleb repeats skeptically. "What was in them?"

"I don't know. Honest. I didn't ask any questions. The first one I just left by the back door of Patsy's at like three in the morning. The next day I heard some people got killed there. I thought it was a weird coincidence."

"Go on."

"Couple days later, I dropped off another little box. At Café Du Monde. This time, I peeked inside it. This little vial. Like the ones they sell on Canal Street, with lavender or tea tree oil. I was nervous, so I went back that night and hung around, just to make sure everything was cool. When I saw those two people start shaking and choking and keel over…I got scared. So I ran."

Caleb folds his arms, not sure how much of this ridiculous story to believe.

"Where did you get these little boxes *from?*"

"All different places. One was in some bushes in an alley in the Lower Ninth. Another was under a stone at the Robert E. Lee statue in Tivoli Circle."

"Who paid you to do this? Who arranged these 'deliveries'?"

Now Mitchell shuts up. He stares at the ground, his feet dancing a little jig.

"I…I don't remember."

It takes Caleb everything he's got to keep from reaching across and strangling the guy. He doesn't even feel the need to get into the third set of murders.

"You know what I think? You're sick in the head. You get off on seeing folks suffer. You're an addict with deep connections to the drug world who could easily get his hands on the synthetic poison found at each scene. You murdered six innocent people for sport. Then you tracked *me* down—the cop coming after you—at my truck, just for the thrill of it."

Caleb rises and marches toward the door. Mitchell tries to stand, too, but jerks forward. His left wrist is handcuffed to the metal table, which is bolted to the ground.

"I didn't know!" Mitchell pleads, his voice cracking with emotion. "I just needed the cash. You gotta believe me!"

"Here's what I believe," Caleb replies. "You're going to rot in jail."

CHAPTER 24

CALEB IS SWEATING BULLETS. His feet hurt like hell. His lower back is on fire.

But he hasn't felt this good in a very long time. Mitchell is behind bars awaiting trial. And there hasn't been another Grim Waiter murder all week.

"Would you hurry up already?" Marlene calls out from the other side of the Killer Chef truck's kitchen. "That catfish is going in somebody's stomach, not out on a date."

Caleb ignores his ex-wife's quip and finishes preparing the final sandwich order of the night as meticulously as all the others. He drizzles precisely ten drops of homemade hot sauce over a fried fillet of catfish. He painstakingly arranges a neat mound of Creole-inspired coleslaw on top. Then he carefully wraps it in paper.

"You know, you bust my chops when I *don't* work hard enough," Caleb says, passing the sandwich to Marlene, who hands it down to their last customer, a middle-aged local musician with a ponytail running down his back and an alto sax case slung over his shoulder. "Now you're giving me a hard time when I *do?*"

"Aw, I'm just kidding, darling," Marlene says, turning off the grill and starting to scrub out the fryer. "I guess I'm just a little tired. Our line hasn't been that long since all that Grim Waiter nonsense first started. Not like I'm complaining or anything."

Caleb tidies up his workstation and then starts doing some dishes. "Food business is back up all around the Quarter," he says. "I don't think *anybody's* complaining."

"Um, excuse me?" A woman's voice is heard from outside the truck.

"Sorry, ma'am," says Marlene without even turning around. "We just closed up."

"That's too bad," the woman replies, raising her voice so Caleb can hear her. "I was hoping your partner could serve up something spicy."

Marlene rolls her eyes, but Caleb grins big. He recognizes that voice right away.

He steps to the cashier window to see Andrea Feldman standing outside. She's wearing a curve-hugging little black dress, her auburn hair is all done up, and her hazel eyes seem to sparkle in the twilight.

"I was just wondering, Detective…now that our case is closed…if you'd care to join me. For a drink. I know a spot in Tremé that makes an old-fashioned that's to die for." She blushes. "Maybe that wasn't the best choice of words."

Caleb smiles, tempted by the invitation. The weeping mess he met last week is gone—replaced by the dangerous, seductive femme fatale he fell hard for the first time.

He looks over at Marlene, who can anticipate exactly what he's about to ask.

"Go. I'll finish the cleanup, do inventory, and lock up. Enjoy yourself. I mean it."

With a grateful nod, Caleb unties his greasy apron and peels off his sweaty T-shirt, throwing on a clean one.

It's not exactly his typical date outfit, but it will have to do.

The rest of his night isn't going to be typical, either.

CHAPTER 25

CALEB SITS BESIDE ANDREA in a cozy booth inside a dim speakeasy. They've just clinked glasses—toasting to "Moving on!"—and taken the first sips of their old-fashioneds.

It's good, Caleb thinks, but certainly not "to die for" like Andrea claimed—a thought that, for a split second, makes his throat tense up. An attractive, professional couple out for a drink, they fit the Grim Waiter's victim profile to a T. But Mitchell is in a holding cell downtown. They're safe.

Right?

A few more seconds pass. When neither he nor Andrea shows any signs of poisoning, Caleb finally exhales. But Andrea is still focused on her drink.

"My apologies, Detective," she says, wrinkling her nose at it. "I remember their recipe being not passable but exceptional. I hope you're not too disappointed."

Refined palate—Caleb appreciates that.

"Not at all," he assures her. "It tastes to me like they

used white sugar instead of brown, and Angostura bitters instead of Peychaud's. But the *company* makes it delicious. By the way, you can call me Caleb."

"In that case, *Caleb*...maybe we should have a nightcap back at my place?"

Caleb doesn't say no. She taps her iPhone, and before he knows it, a black SUV is pulling up outside. As they slide into the leather backseat, Caleb feels a little jittery, like they're back in high school. And he likes it.

As they walk up the pathway to her massive violet-hued mansion, a gust of wind whips off the Mississippi and sends a chill up his spine.

Caleb hesitates again.

Part of him considers giving Andrea a gentlemanly peck on the cheek and heading home. But there's something about this woman—the way she smells, the way she talks, the way her hips move—that is just too enticing to turn down. And when she whispers, "There's a special room upstairs I want to show you," Caleb's curiosity gets the best of him.

They make their way through the familiar Degas-lined hallway, then up a spiral staircase to the second floor. Andrea opens a door to reveal a spacious parlor that's utterly different from the refined elegance of the rest of the house.

It has a pool table. A giant flat-screen television. An L-shaped wet bar. And it's filled with sports memorabilia, especially from the University of Wisconsin. An oversized Bucky Badger stuffed mascot is even perched on one of the bar stools.

"You didn't tell me you had a man cave," Caleb exclaims, taking the place in. If he had any doubts that Andrea was basically the perfect woman, he doesn't anymore. "What's with all the Badger stuff?"

"It's where I went to college," Andrea explains, stepping behind the bar and pouring them each two fingers of top-shelf bourbon. "I'd never been to a single sporting event in my life...until I started dating the quarterback. Our relationship didn't survive, but my love of Wisconsin football did. Why are you giving me that look?"

Andrea hands Caleb his drink, but he places it right back down on the bar and embraces her.

The moment their lips meet, they both give in completely. They half-walk, half-grope their way into the bedroom, leaving a trail of clothing in their wake.

When it's all over, Andrea falls asleep almost at once.

Caleb doesn't.

It was a fun night, no doubt about it. But as he lies there next to her, wide-awake for nearly an hour before deciding to slip out, something just doesn't feel quite right.

CHAPTER 26

DOROTHY *NEVER* STEPS foot out of her natural habitat: the dim maze of colorful wires and flickering computer monitors on the third floor of NOPD headquarters.

Which is why when Caleb spots her walking through the detectives' bullpen on the first floor carrying a laptop, he knows right away that something big is up.

"Isn't this a nice surprise," he says as she approaches his desk. "I wish I'd known you were coming, Dorothy. I would have bought some pastries and coffee, like always."

"Save that buttering up for some bread," she quips, setting her laptop on his desk and firing it up. As before, her fingers move around the keyboard so fast they practically blur. "You know how Albatross-Gomez isn't cooperating with prosecutors?"

"Right," Caleb says. "I'd love to know if he had accomplices, who his poison supplier was, all that stuff. But I heard he's not talking much. Then again, he's facing six life sentences, possibly even the needle. I don't blame him for pleading the fifth."

"Well, he may not *need* to speak after all. Take a look at this."

She spins her computer screen around to reveal streams of numbers and data, indecipherable to a layman like Caleb.

"What exactly am I looking at?"

Dorothy explains that her team has been combing through the victims' cell phones for nearly a week now, looking for any suspicious activity, or anything that might link them back to Albatross-Gomez. But they've only had access to *five* of the victims' phone records. Until now.

"Jonah Leach, the man killed at Clancy's, didn't send texts or make calls in the usual way," Dorothy explains. "He worked as a venture capitalist and dealt with sensitive information all the time, so he only communicated via an app called iScramble. It digitally encrypts all text and voice messages, both incoming and outgoing, and makes accessing traditional phone records virtually impossible."

Caleb nods, understanding where Dorothy is going with this. "*Virtually* impossible. So I assume *you've* just found a way to decrypt it?"

"Exactly. I broke the hex-encryption key myself, thank you very much. We have hundreds of calls and thousands of texts to sift through. Here are some of the numbers that came up recently, in order of frequency."

She points to a spreadsheet on her laptop screen. It's a phone number beginning with the 504 New Orleans code.

Caleb considers the number. It feels eerily familiar. He types it into his own phone's keypad to see if it matches any of his contacts. "Oh, shit…" he mumbles when a name comes up.

"Wow. It's…it's Andrea Feldman's cell! Martin Feldman's ex-wife."

Dorothy nods grimly, apparently not surprised that Caleb and Andrea have a personal relationship.

"Well, those two shared some racy messages over the last few months. Until a few weeks ago, when Jonah tried to end the relationship. And Andrea didn't take it very well at all."

Caleb is speechless, shaken to his core. Andrea has been romantically involved with all three of the Grim Waiter's male victims. Of course it can't just be a coincidence. She *must* be somehow involved. But how? Is she being punished vicariously, forced to watch three ex-lovers be killed? Or is *she* the one doing the killing?

There's only one way to find out.

CHAPTER 27

PATIENCE IS ONE of Caleb's strong suits. Whether waiting for a ball of dough to rise or a suspect to slip up, he has a knack for staying calm and determined, no matter the circumstances.

But right now? That patience is being put to the test.

Driving an unmarked vehicle from the police pool, Caleb has been parked down the block from Château Feldman for the better part of forty-eight hours, keeping an eye out for Andrea.

The detective in him is hoping he can catch her in the act and link her back to the murders.

But the red-blooded man in him is praying she's innocent, that there must be some explanation, that the woman he has feelings for isn't also a ruthless killer.

After two days of zero movement inside or outside Andrea's palatial home, at around ten o'clock on the second night of Caleb's stakeout he sees a woman jogging across the front yard...wearing a Wisconsin Badgers hat. Not an everyday sight here in New Orleans.

It's dark, making it difficult to distinguish her shape, but there's no doubt in his mind it's Andrea.

Steeling himself, Caleb slips on a nondescript dark baseball cap of his own, gets out of his sedan, and discreetly starts to follow her.

He jogs behind Andrea without being seen for nearly a quarter of a mile. But he's thrown for a loop when they pass the stately old Ursuline Convent and the Beauregard-Keyes House—a small, southern version of the White House painted canary-yellow.

The jogging route Andrea is taking is unusual. But Caleb stays on her tail, despite her brisk pace. He debates calling out to her, pretending that he was out for an evening run, too.

But something tells him not to. Something tells him to see where Andrea goes.

When they reach St. Philip Street, it finally hits him.

Andrea is running right toward the Killer Chef truck.

Because he's been on the stakeout tonight, Marlene is working it alone. Caleb is supposed to be there, by her side, cracking jokes, helping her shut the place down and keeping her safe. If he doesn't get there fast, who knows what—

"Shit!" Caleb cries out as he trips over a loose piece of concrete in the sidewalk and tumbles forward to the ground, hard. Of all the times to be clumsy.

He picks himself back up as quickly as he can…but when he looks around, he realizes Andrea is gone.

This isn't good. Caleb starts running again. His only thought is to get to the truck, fast.

CHAPTER 28

CALEB'S LUNGS ARE BURNING when he reaches the Killer Chef truck.

He slows and approaches quietly, with great caution. The side panel is already down, covering the cashier and takeout windows, preventing him from seeing inside. The truck's rear door is closed, too—strange, because Marlene typically leaves it ajar, especially when she's working alone.

Caleb can just sense it: *something isn't right*.

He considers calling for backup, but in a situation like this, every second counts. He doesn't want to spook Andrea, either, and make her do something she doesn't mean to.

Slowly, carefully, Caleb creeps closer toward the truck.

He stops near the rear stairs when he hears a commotion of some sort going on inside. Even with no knowledge of what's happening, he has to act. Now.

Caleb draws his sidearm and flips off the safety. Cautiously he reaches for the rear door's handle. Finding it unlocked, he turns it and pushes it open.

CHAPTER 29

THERE SHE IS, her back to him, wearing that Wisconsin Badgers cap—and by her stance and his view of a trembling Marlene, she appears to be wielding a knife.

But it's not Andrea standing there with her back to him…it's *Patsy*.

What the hell is this?

Standing just a few feet behind her, Caleb's first instinct is to tackle Patsy and take her down. But he decides to make no sudden movements at all. He doesn't even want to make eye contact with Marlene, since it might clue Patsy in that he's there.

"I wear my heart on my sleeve, Marlene," Patsy replies, her voice cracking with pain. "When I fall, I fall *hard*." She sniffles. "I fell in love with him. And he dumped me. That was hard enough. Then he paraded his *other* girlfriend all over town!"

Caleb is still standing frozen, afraid to move a muscle, unsure what to do next.

"So why are you here?" Marlene asks. "Why now?"

"Shut up, you bitch!" Patsy screams, waving her knife wildly. "Like you don't know. This is about *Caleb*. After that night of the deaths—it was so obvious to me that you two were still in love. Admit it. Admit it, damn it!"

Caleb debates taking a step closer, but he just can't bring himself to risk it.

"Do you think I like working late nights here, alone, while the love of my life is off playing Dick Tracy?" Marlene asks.

Caleb watches as her face tightens with what looks like real pain.

"He broke *both* of our hearts, Patsy. I probably hate the piece of shit even more than you do. You guys only dated. Us? We tied the knot. And he still couldn't be faithful. He's a real bastard."

Patsy seems to pause at Marlene's words. So does Caleb. And they feel like a sharp knife to his gut. Is his ex-wife just acting? Or does she really mean some of that?

"I can show you where he keeps his jalapeños," Marlene says, her eyes lighting up with evil mischief. "Let me get them for you. A little poison—"

"Don't move!" Patsy snaps. "I'll get them. Where are they?"

"There," Marlene says. "That metal jar on the counter."

Keeping her knife aimed at Marlene, Patsy slowly approaches the counter and reaches out for the metal container. But as soon as she touches it—

"Ouch!" she shouts—since it's actually holding the formerly scalding-hot oil from the deep fryer. Her hand recoils from the burn and Caleb sees her grip on her knife loosen—

And he takes his chance, lunging at Patsy from behind.

She's caught completely by surprise but instantly wriggles to escape, stronger than Caleb would have thought.

They struggle and grapple in the tiny kitchen, knocking over pots and cooking trays, until finally Caleb manages to knock the knife from her hand and pin her arms behind her back.

"Get off of me!" she shouts, but Caleb ignores her and slaps on some handcuffs.

"It was *you,* Patsy?" he demands. "All this time? I did love you, it's true…but what the hell is wrong with you?"

Patsy doesn't answer. Instead, her lip begins to tremble and tears start to stream down her cheeks.

Caleb already has his phone out and is dialing for backup. He scoops up Patsy's knife, then embraces Marlene. Her tough-gal facade from moments ago has completely vanished. Now she's shaking in his arms, flooded with a rush of emotion.

"Good thinking with that grease can," he says, stroking her hair.

"Good thinking sneaking into the truck. If you hadn't shown up…"

Caleb shushes Marlene and continues to hold her tight. In the distance, they hear police sirens.

"I didn't *actually* want to kill you, you know," Marlene says. Then, to Caleb's delight, her signature sarcasm starts creeping back. "I mean, I thought about it before, don't get me wrong. But then I'd have to hire someone to cover your shifts, and it's so hard to find good help sometimes."

Caleb smirks. Now that Marlene is herself again, he turns his attention back to Patsy.

"Why'd you do it, Patz? Kill all those people? Poison in your own restauraunt?"

"What?" she says. She looks at him with shock that seems genuine. "I didn't!"

What? He knows her so well—but not what she's capable of.

Suddenly, Caleb remembers. The chase that brought him here. "Where did you get that hat, Patsy?"

"The…oh, this hat. From Tariq."

"Tariq *Bishar?*" Caleb asks, surprised.

"I'd seen your car near Andrea Feldman's house. So I went there…but ran into him. He said I was in the wrong place."

She paused.

"He…knew I was angry with you. He's at the restaurant a lot.

"He gave me the hat and said that I should disguise myself and get close. I'm so sorry, Marlene…I guess I just got so angry once I was here and saw you…I was really mad at Caleb."

But Caleb is already out the door.

CHAPTER 30

CALEB THOUGHT HE'D been sprinting before, but now he charges down the street as if his life depends on it. Lungs burning and muscles screaming, he curses himself for having left his post at Andrea's house.

It seems like hours when he rounds the back of the mansion, slowing to catch his breath and silently creep toward the door. There's no movement at the windows. Fleetingly Caleb thinks about calling for backup, but there's no time to lose.

Finding the French doors to the patio unlocked, he eases one open and steps inside. It's silent. He tiptoes to the central hall, with the ballerina paintings on the walls, making for the stairs. But rounding to the staircase, he hears a muffled sob.

There, in the sitting room he's now facing, is Andrea. With a gun to her head.

"Oh, hello, Caleb," says Tariq, with his customary shit-eating grin. He stands protectively behind Andrea, who sits in a chair, trembling. One hand covers her mouth and the other holds the gun. "I had a feeling you'd turn up here. But it's too late for you to do anything now."

"Put the gun down, Tariq. Step away from Andrea."

"So you care about Andrea now, do you?" Tariq says, a dangerous glint in his eye. "Where were you when she was being criminally neglected and abused by her joke of a husband? Or led along by that crook, Brent? Or that swindler, Jonah? All unfaithful. All a disgrace to this city."

"Did you kill them, Tariq? And then try to frame Albatross-Gomez? But it was you who added the poison to their dishes. You killed them, didn't you?" Caleb tries to maintain eye contact, hoping to push Tariq into doing something sloppy. "You did, Killer Chef. Or so the headlines will say. *Killer Chef Tastes His Own Recipe?* Case Closed."

Tariq raises the gun and points it directly at Caleb's face.

"Don't, Tariq!" Andrea shouts.

He looks down at her, gun still leveled at Caleb. "He's no good for you."

"He's nothing to me. I want to be with you—but we need to get out of here fast. The police will be here any moment."

"You saved my life. But we need to go."

Andrea grabs Tariq's hand, pulling him down for a kiss. Caught off-guard, he leans in but then pulls back, remembering the gun, the final act.

But it's too late. Caleb lunges across the room, knocking Tariq down and the gun out of his hand.

As he pushes Tariq roughly down on the ground, he realizes in a panic that his handcuffs are still on Patsy.

But then, in a moment of sudden calm, he registers the sweet sound of sirens coming closer and closer.

CHAPTER 31

FOR THE SECOND TIME in an hour, Caleb holds a woman in shock. But this time he needs the comforting as much as she does.

"I can't believe I didn't see it sooner. Tariq has access to every kitchen in the city. And he knows every bit of gossip when it comes to the rich and famous: every debt, every feud, every affair. But I don't understand. Why did he fixate on you?"

Andrea is holding him tightly. "I saw him at parties…and he'd read my books. I used to get fan letters from a stalker, always signed 'the Loving Tarantula,' but I never made the connection. He and Marty once had a public battle over some luxury apartments Marty refused to knock out public housing for. I never thought it would come to this…."

Marlene rushes into the room, now filled with police waiting to take statements. Never a favorite with the New Orleans Police Department, Tariq has been handcuffed and unceremoniously thrown into a squad car.

"Caleb! My God! You scared me half to death, left me with that crazy woman, and now I find out you're chasing down a madman all by yourself...."

Caleb smiles broadly at his two favorite women. "What do you say when all this is over, I whip us up a couple killer sandwiches and we go listen to a little jazz?"

Marlene smiles and nods at Andrea. "I think that sounds like the perfect end to a crazy night."

Someone wants to make his first big case his last

Read on for an extract

THE WEATHERMAN NAILED IT. "Sticky, hot, and miserable. Highs in the nineties. Stay inside if you can."

I can't. I have to get someplace. Fast.

Jesus Christ, it's hot. Especially if you're running as fast as you can through Central Park *and* you're wearing a dark gray Armani silk suit, a light gray Canali silk shirt, and black Ferragamo shoes.

As you might have guessed, I am late—very, very late. *Très en retard,* as we say in France.

I pick up speed until my legs hurt. I can feel little blisters forming on my toes and heels.

Why did I ever come to New York?

Why, oh why, did I leave Paris?

If I were running like this in Paris, I would be stopping all traffic. I would be the center of attention. Men and women would be shouting for the police.

"A young businessman has gone berserk! He is shoving baby carriages out of his path. He is frightening the old ladies walking their dogs."

But this is not Paris. This is New York.

So forget it. Even the craziest event in New York goes unnoticed. The dog walkers keep on walking their dogs. The teenage lovers kiss. A toddler points to me. His mother glances up. Then she shrugs.

Will even one New Yorker dial 911? Or 311?

Forget about that also. You see, I am part of the police. A French detective now working with the Seventeenth Precinct on my specialty—drug smuggling, drug sales, and drug-related homicides.

My talent for being late has, in a mere two months, become almost legendary with my colleagues in the precinct house. But... oh, *merde*...showing up late for today's meticulously planned stakeout on Madison Avenue and 71st Street will do nothing to help my reputation, a reputation as an uncooperative rich French kid, a rebel with too many causes.

Merde...today of all days I should have known better than to wake my gorgeous girlfriend to say good-bye.

"I cannot be late for this one, Dalia."

"Just one more good-bye squeeze. What if you're shot and I never see you again?"

The good-bye "squeeze" turned out to be significantly longer than I had planned.

Eh. It doesn't matter. I'm where I'm supposed to be now. A mere forty-five minutes late.

MY PARTNER, DETECTIVE Maria Martinez, is seated on the driver's side of an unmarked police car at 71st Street and Madison Avenue.

While keeping her eyes on the surrounding area, Maria unlocks the passenger door. I slide in, drowning in perspiration. She glances at me for a second, then speaks.

"Man. What's the deal? Did you put your suit on first and *then* take your shower?"

"Funny," I say. "Sorry I'm late."

"You should have little business cards with that phrase on it—'Sorry I'm late.'"

I'm certain that Maria Martinez doesn't care whether I'm late. Unlike a lot of my detective colleagues, she doesn't mind that I'm not big on "protocol." I'm late a lot. I do a lot of careless things. I bring ammo for a Glock 22 when I'm packing a Glock 27. I like a glass or two of white wine with lunch…it's a long list. But Maria overlooks most of it.

My other idiosyncrasies she has come to accept, more or less. I must have a proper *déjeuner*. That's lunch. No mere sandwich will do. What's more, a glass or two of good wine never did anything but enhance the flavor of a lunch.

You see, Maria "gets" me. Even better, she knows what I know:

together we're a cool combination of her procedure-driven meth-ods and my purely instinct-driven methods.

"So where are we with this bust?" I say.

"We're still sitting on our butts. That's where we are," she says. Then she gives details.

"They got two pairs of cops on the other side of the street, and two other detectives—Imani Williams and Henry Whatever-the-Hell-His-Long-Polish-Name-Is—at the end of the block. That team'll go into the garage.

"Then there's another team behind the garage. They'll hold back and *then* go into the garage.

"Then they got three guys on the roof of the target building."

The target building is a large former town house that's now home to a store called Taylor Antiquities. It's a place filled with the fancy antique pieces lusted after by trust-fund babies and hedge-fund hotshots. Maria and I have already cased Taylor Antiquities a few times. It's a store where you can lay down your Amex Cen-turion card and walk away with a white jade vase from the Yuan dynasty or purchase the four-poster bed where John and Abigail Adams reportedly conceived little John Quincy.

"And what about us?"

"Our assignment spot is inside the store," she says.

"No. I want to be where the action is," I say.

"Be careful what you wish for," Maria says. "Do what they tell you. We're inside the store. Over and out. Meanwhile, how about watching the street with me?"

Maria Martinez is total cop. At the moment she is heart-and-soul into the surveillance. Her eyes dart from the east side of the street to the west. Every few seconds, she glances into the rearview mirror. Follows it with a quick look into the side-view mirror. Searches straight ahead. Then she does it all over again.

Me? Well, I'm looking around, but I'm also wondering if I can take a minute off to grab a cardboard cup of lousy American coffee.

Don't get me wrong. And don't be put off by what I said about my impatience with "procedure." No. I am very cool with being a detective. In fact, I've wanted to be a detective since I was four years old. I'm also very good at my job. And I've got the résumé to prove it.

Last year in Pigalle, one of the roughest parts of Paris, I solved a drug-related gang homicide and made three on-the-scene arrests. Just me and a twenty-five-year-old traffic cop.

I was happy. I was successful. For a few days I was even famous.

The next morning the name Luc Moncrief was all over the newspapers and the Internet. A rough translation of the headline on the front page of *Le Monde*:

OLDEST PIGALLE DRUG GANG SMASHED BY YOUNGEST PARIS DETECTIVE— LUC MONCRIEF

Underneath was this subhead:

Parisian Heartthrob Hauls in Pigalle Drug Lords

The paparazzi had always been somewhat interested in whom I was dating; after that, they were obsessed. Club owners comped my table with bottles of Perrier-Jouët Champagne. Even my father, the chairman of a giant pharmaceuticals company, gave me one of his rare compliments.

"Very nice job…for a playboy. Now I hope you've got this 'detective thing' out of your system."

I told him thank you, but I did not tell him that "this detective thing" was not out of my system. Or that I enjoyed the very generous monthly allowance that he gave me too much.

So when my *capitaine supérieur* announced that the NYPD wanted to trade one of their art-forgery detectives for one of our Paris drug enforcement detectives for a few months, I jumped at the offer. From my point of view, it was a chance to reconnect with my former lover, Dalia Boaz. From my Parisian *lieutenant* point of view, it was an opportunity to add some needed discipline and learning to my instinctive approach to detective work.

So here I am. On Madison Avenue, my eyes are burning with sweat. I can actually feel the perspiration squishing around in my shoes.

Detective Martinez remains focused completely on the street scene. But God, I need some coffee, some air. I begin speaking.

"Listen. If I could just jump out for a minute and—"

As I'm about to finish the sentence, two vans—one black, one red—turn into the garage next door to Taylor Antiquities.

Our cell phones automatically buzz with a loud sirenlike sound. The doors of the unmarked police cars begin to open.

As Maria and I hit the street, she speaks.

"It looks like our evidence has finally arrived."

JAMES PATTERSON
BOOK**SHOTS**
OUT THIS MONTH

KILLER CHEF

Someone is poisoning the diners in New Orleans' best restaurants. Now it's up to chef and homicide cop Caleb Rooney to catch a killer set on revenge.

DAZZLING: THE DIAMOND TRILOGY, PART 1

To support her artistic career, Siobhan Dempsey works at the elite Stone Room in New York City... never expecting to be swept away by tech billionaire Derick Miller.

BODYGUARD

Special Agent Abbie Whitmore has only one task: protect Congressman Jonathan Lassiter from a violent cartel's threats. Yet she's never had to do it while falling in love...

JAMES
PATTERSON
BOOK**SHOTS**
COMING SOON

THE CHRISTMAS MYSTERY

Two priceless paintings disappear from a Park Avenue murder scene –
French detective Luc Moncrief is in for a not-so-merry Christmas.

COME AND GET US

Miranda Cooper's life takes a terrifying turn when an SUV deliberately
runs her and her husband off a desolate Arizona road.

RADIANT: THE DIAMOND TRILOGY, PART 2

Siobhan has moved to Detroit following her traumatic break-up
with Derick, but when Derick comes after her, Siobhan must decide
whether she can trust him again...

HOT WINTER NIGHTS

Allie Fairchild made a mistake when she moved to Montana, but just
when she's about to throw in the towel, life in Bear Mountain takes a
surprisingly sexy turn...

BOOK**SHOTS**

STORIES AT THE SPEED OF LIFE

www.bookshots.com

ALSO BY JAMES PATTERSON

Private India (*with Ashwin Sanghi*)
Private Vegas (*with Maxine Paetro*)
Private Sydney (*with Kathryn Fox*)
Private Paris (*with Mark Sullivan*)
The Games (*with Mark Sullivan*)

NYPD RED SERIES
NYPD Red (*with Marshall Karp*)
NYPD Red 2 (*with Marshall Karp*)
NYPD Red 3 (*with Marshall Karp*)
NYPD Red 4 (*with Marshall Karp*)

STAND-ALONE THRILLERS
Sail (*with Howard Roughan*)
Swimsuit (*with Maxine Paetro*)
Don't Blink (*with Howard Roughan*)
Postcard Killers (*with Liza Marklund*)
Toys (*with Neil McMahon*)
Now You See Her (*with Michael Ledwidge*)
Kill Me If You Can (*with Marshall Karp*)
Guilty Wives (*with David Ellis*)
Zoo (*with Michael Ledwidge*)
Second Honeymoon (*with Howard Roughan*)
Mistress (*with David Ellis*)
Invisible (*with David Ellis*)
The Thomas Berryman Number
Truth or Die (*with Howard Roughan*)

Murder House (*with David Ellis*)
Never Never (*with Candice Fox*)
Woman of God (*with Maxine Paetro*)

BOOKSHOTS
Black & Blue (*with Candice Fox*)
Break Point (*with Lee Stone*)
Cross Kill
Private Royals (*with Rees Jones*)
The Hostage (*with Robert Gold*)
Zoo 2 (*with Max DiLallo*)
Heist (*with Rees Jones*)
Hunted (*with Andrew Holmes*)
Airport: Code Red (*with Michael White*)
The Trial (*with Maxine Paetro*)
Little Black Dress (*with Emily Raymond*)
Chase (*with Michael Ledwidge*)
Let's Play Make-Believe (*with James O. Born*)
Dead Heat (*with Lee Stone*)
Triple Threat
113 Minutes (*with Max DiLallo*)
The Verdict (*with Robert Gold*)
French Kiss (*with Richard DiLallo*)
$10,000,000 Marriage Proposal (*with Hilary Liftin*)
Kill or Be Killed